Lost American Fiction

Edited by Matthew J. Bruccoli

The title for this series, Lost American Fiction, is unsatisfactory. A more accurate series title would be "Forgotten Works of American Fiction That Deserve a New Public"—which states the rationale for reprinting these titles. No claim is made that we are resuscitating lost masterpieces, although at least two of the titles may well qualify. We are reprinting works that merit re-reading because they are now social or literary documents—or just because they are good writing. It isn't really that simple, of course, for Southern Illinois University Press is a scholarly publisher; and we have serious ambitions for the series. We expect that "Lost American Fiction" will revive some books and authors from undeserved obscurity and that the series will therefore plug some of the holes in American literary history. Of course, we hope to find an occasional lost masterpiece.

Ten titles have been published in the series, with three more in production. The response has been encouraging. We are gratified that many readers share our conviction that one of the proper functions of a university press is to rescue good writing from oblivion.

M. J. B.

MR *and* MRS HADDOCK
Abroad ❧ ❧ ❧ ❧ ❧ ❧
DONALD OGDEN STEWART

A TUGBOAT PUT OUT FROM THE SHIP'S SIDE

MR *and* MRS HADDOCK
ABROAD

By
DONALD OGDEN STEWART

With an Afterword
by the Author

Illustrations by Herb Roth

SOUTHERN ILLINOIS UNIVERSITY PRESS
Carbondale and Edwardsville

Feffer & Simons, Inc.
London and Amsterdam

Library of Congress Cataloging in Publication Data

Stewart, Donald Ogden
    Mr and Mrs Haddock abroad.
    (Lost American fiction)
    Reprint of the ed. published by G. H. Doran Co.,
New York.
    I. Title.
PZ3.S8498Mi8 [PS3537.T485] 813'.5'2 75-6555
ISBN 0-8093-0731-6

To
ANNE STEWART OUTHWAITE — D. O. S.'s sister
and
CHARLES PEABODY OUTHWAITE
with affection and gratitude

MR *and* MRS HADDOCK
Abroad

MR *and* MRS HADDOCK
ABROAD

CHAPTER I

Mr and Mrs Haddock were very excited about going abroad. It was the first time either of them had ever been abroad to Europe, although Mr Haddock had been to Chicago eight times, Kansas City five times, Kansas City (Kan.) five times, St. Louis four times, Denver four times, and New York City twice, but it had rained four days out of five.

Mrs Haddock had been to St. Louis once and Chicago twice, in Pullman cars, named, respectively, Edgar Allen Poe, Sweet Juniper, and Spauldingopolis. She had not slept very well the first two times and the third time she had not slept at all. She slept very well at home, though, mostly on her back and left

[11]

side. Her mother's maiden name had been Quetch.

Mr and Mrs Haddock had been married twenty-four odd years and their grandparents were all dead on both sides. So they were quite alone in the world except for Mr Haddock's father and mother and Mrs Haddock's father and mother, who were, however, quite old, their combined ages totalling 439 or several score years.

They also had a son, Frank Haddock, but he wasn't going abroad, although he could have gone abroad if he had wanted to, but he didn't want to, and they also had a young daughter Mildred.

That ought to give you a pretty fair idea of the city in which Mr and Mrs Haddock lived. It was called Legion, being named after an old Indian squaw called Legion, who was said to have been buried there originally.

When Mr Haddock and Mrs Haddock had been first married he had said to a lot of their best friends:

"You may sneer at us now for only going

to the Mammoth Cave, Kentucky, on our wedding journey but some day you will sneer out
of the other side of your mouth."

And with that he had hit his horse a terrific
slash and driven away, and he and she had
sworn that very day that before they were
forty they would show everybody and go
abroad. Mr Haddock was now fifty-one and
Mrs Haddock was forty-nine and so their
prophecy had come true. They were going
abroad.

"Do you think the silver will be safe?" had
been Mrs Haddock's anxious question each
year when Mr Haddock had proposed a trip
to Europe, and Mr Haddock each year had
sadly shaken his head and said "No."

But this year, instead of answering "No" he
had replied:

"We could put it in a safe deposit box in
some bank," and so that problem had been
finally solved.

There were, however, other problems which
confronted the prospective travellers.

There was, first of all, the problem of Mildred. Mildred was Mr and Mrs Haddock's ten year old daughter who had come to them late in life but was having her teeth straightened by Dr. Hawley.

"This trip abroad will be so wonderful for Mildred," said Mrs Haddock.

"And for the people with whom she comes in contact," added a voice, but Mrs Haddock had gone. It was Mr Marsden, Mildred's Sunday School teacher, so that on his otherwise pleasant face was no mean snarl.

Then there was the age old problem of where to go.

"Paris?" suggested Mr Haddock, a little hopefully.

"The Dickens' country," said Mrs Haddock, who liked all of Dickens except "Bleak House" and parts of "Great Expectations," "Barnaby Rudge," "Oliver Twist," and "Vanity Fair."

The very next day Mr Haddock had another idea:

"I tell you where let's go," he said, "Paris."

"We can't speak French," replied Mrs

Haddock, "but of course we ought to go to Paris. Won't it be wonderful to really see Notre Dame."

"And the Sewers," said Mr Haddock. "And, besides, Mildred can speak French."

"Beautifully," added Mrs Haddock. "You ought to hear what Miss Spencer says, Will."

A few days later Mr Haddock said "Rome."

"The Catacombs," said Mrs Haddock.

"Venice," said Mr Haddock.

"Gondolas," said Mrs Haddock. "Will, I think you had really better take your heavy overcoat."

And so one by one the more important problems were disposed of.

"I think I ought to get a note book," said Mrs Haddock.

So she made a note on a piece of paper, "Get note book," and lost the piece of paper but got the note book at Bromfield's where they had had an account for many years.

"We are going abroad," she said to the clerk.

[15]

"My," said the clerk, "I certainly envy you."

So the note book was called "My Trip Abroad" and in front were a number of interesting pages devoted to the population of cities (1900) and how to change from Fahrenheit to Centigrade and back again when it was hot, and what the different Storm and Distress signals were in International Navigation. It also had a useful Comparative Money Table for Travellers which showed that one German mark was worth a little over 24 cents in American money.

"It says here, Will," said Mrs Haddock, "that one German mark is worth a little over 24 cents in American money."

"Does it?" replied Mr Haddock and that was all that was ever said about the German mark.

Then too "My Trip Abroad" had a large folded map of the World on which was a black cross showing the exact spot where the "Titanic" had sunk. One night Mrs Haddock blotted out that cross so that no one could

Mr and Mrs Haddock Abroad

tell what it was for, unless little Mildred told them. Little Mildred always told them.

"That blot," said little Mildred, "is where the 'Titanic' sank. There used to be a cross there but mother blotted it out. Two thousand three hundred and fifty-eight lives were lost."

It was very difficult to fool little Mildred about anything.

In another part of Mrs Haddock's note book were several blank pages entitled "Places Visited and Interesting People Met," and there was one whole page for the "Captain's Signature."

"I can hardly wait until we get on the boat," said Mrs Haddock, and she filled both her fountain pens very full of ink and got most of it off her fingers by using the pumice stone in the upstairs bathroom.

Many of Mrs Haddock's friends had been abroad once and from them she obtained much useful information which she put in her book under the head of "Notes—Miscellaneous" as for example:

[17]

Mr and Mrs Haddock Abroad

PARIS—*H.K.W.* says French laundries reasonable but make list. Chemise is a shirt in French. No starch best. Notre Dame best by moonlight. Evenings cool (Will—overcoat). Paris well lighted. Take full ½ day for Louvre. Venus de Milo on first floor. Good Corsets (Cora) at "Au Printemps" near Opera pronounced Oh Prantom. French hard to understand. Don't let Will shout. Mona Lisa on second floor. Elevator—tip. Stairs not hard. Don't touch with white gloves. Louvre free on Sunday. Good Presb. church near Arc de Triumph. Notre Dame catholic.

Cora says Notre Dame best in morning and always check up on waiters about the bill. Bill is addition, waiter garçon but pronounced differently. Bread dirty. Versailles—fountains play once a month. Don't drink French water. Vin blanc a good white wine. Will's acid. Can get good Bicarb. Soda in Paris on Rue de la Paix. French meals different. Will's pills. Napoleon's tomb sure.

Aunt Flora says Notre Dame best in after-

noon. Always rains in morning. Damp—
unhealthy. Hotels not well heated. Cotton
sheets. French not clean. Always rains in
evening. Eiffel Tower unsafe. Morgue gone.
French men unsafe. French immoral. No
bathtubs. Catholics. Mrs Gueminder saw
bugs.

"I'm so excited," said Mrs Haddock as the
time for departure drew near. "I've never
been on a boat before."

"You'll be very seasick," said Aunt Flora.
"The Quetches were never good sailors except
your half-brother Edmund who was drowned
at that picnic thirteen years ago next July
fourth."

"Drowned people can be raised to the surface by firing guns over a river," said little
Mildred.

"People who are drowned at sea," said Aunt
Flora, "are never recovered."

"I should think," said little Mildred, "that
if you fired a big enough gun over the Atlan-

tic Ocean you could bring a lot of interesting things to the surface."

That was the way little Mildred's mind worked and she was already becoming known among the simple folk of the town as the Joan of Arc of 453 Crestview Avenue.

The last week before sailing was full of problems. There was first of all the question of whether or not to take Mr Haddock's winter pajamas.

"It might turn cold," said Mrs Haddock, who, man and boy, had had forty-nine years of experience with weather and ought to have known what she was talking about.

"Nonsense," said Mr Haddock. "It won't turn cold in June."

"It was in June," said Aunt Flora, "that your brother Samuel took pneumonia and died—June twenty-sixth."

"That wasn't in Europe," said Mr Haddock, who had once thought of taking up the law.

"Weather is the same the world over," said Mrs Haddock.

"It isn't," said Mildred. "In Abyssinia the average mean rainfall is 13.4 inches."

"But we aren't going to Abyssinia," said Mr Haddock plaintively.

"We might," said Mrs Haddock, and so she packed the pajamas rather triumphantly (for pajamas) and asked Mr Haddock to sit on the lid.

"I don't see why you packed my dress suit," said Mr Haddock. "I'm not going to any banquets."

"At the Opera in Paris," said little Mildred, "full evening dress is *de rigueur.*"

"You see," said Mrs Haddock. "Mildred, talk some more French for your Aunt Flora."

"I won't," said Mildred.

"Please, Mildred," said Aunt Flora, "talk some French for your Aunt Flora."

"Mildred," said Mr Haddock, "you talk some French for your Aunt Flora or you don't get any Toasted Fruito for dessert tonight. Papa means it."

"All right," said Mildred. "Où est l'encre?"

"You see," said Mrs Haddock proudly.

"What does that mean, Mildred?" asked Aunt Flora.

"Where is the ink?" translated Mildred obediently with a pretty toss of her curls.

"She will be a great help to you," said Aunt Flora.

"Especially if we need much ink," said Mr Haddock.

"I'm sure we are taking enough," said Mrs Haddock, but she opened the trunk once more to be sure, for she had never gotten over the time she and Mr Haddock had been caught in St. Louis without any library paste.

"This is our passport," said Mr Haddock, and he spoke the truth.

"I hope you don't lose it," said Aunt Flora.

"The passport picture didn't turn out very well," said Mrs Haddock, "do you think?"

"No" said Aunt Flora. "The picture is awful. You look eighty, Will. And Mildred looks like a negro."

"Maybe I have some negro blood in me," said Mildred. "I read a story once——"

"Mildred," said her mother, "I thought I heard some one knocking at the back door."

So Mildred went down the back stairs into the kitchen, which at that time happened to be in the rear of the house.

"She shouldn't be allowed to read such stories," said Aunt Flora, who heartily disapproved of the intermarriage of whites and blacks.

"She isn't," said Mrs Haddock. "But the best way is not to scold her. When she comes back she will have forgotten all about it."

In a few minutes Mildred came back.

"There wasn't any one at all," she said, and then she added, "That story I read was about a white woman who——"

"Mildred!" said her father, severely, for in questions involving miscegenation Mr Haddock could be very severe, and so the subject was dropped until Mildred might care to bring it up again.

Finally the day for their departure came and went and the next morning they found themselves on a train approaching New York.

[23]

"Are we on time, George?" asked Mr Haddock genially to the porter as he (Mr Haddock) climbed down from his comfortable upper berth where he had slept part of the night.

"Yes suh," replied George, who had been christened David Farragut after David Farragut. "I callate as how we is."

"Good," said Mr Haddock, and he went forward into the washroom but it was the ladies' washroom, so he came back to his berth and this time after a moment's thought he went in exactly the opposite direction and soon he was in the gentlemen's washroom.

"Always room for one more, brother," said a nice jolly fat gentleman who was brushing his teeth and part of his left ear in order to battle pyorrhea.

Soon Mr Haddock was engaged in the process of washing, for which purpose he used water, soap and towels, so that by the time he had finished only he and the fat gentleman were left in the washroom.

"I see you're going abroad," said the fat

gentleman looking at the steamer label "Cabin Baggage" which Mrs Haddock had carefully pasted on Mr Haddock's bag.

"Yes," said Mr Haddock. "I thought I would take my wife and daughter over."

"You first trip?" asked the other, whom, for want of a worse name, we will call Leslie J. Sills.

"Yes," said Mr Haddock, hanging his head partly in shame and partly because he had dropped his collar button on the floor and wanted to look for it.

"I've been across," said Mr Sills, not without pride.

"Were you sick?" asked Mr Haddock, not without anxiety.

"Only the first four days," said Mr Sills.

"Oh," said Mr Haddock, relieved.

"You won't be very sick," said Mr Sills, "unless you have a rough crossing. It's often rough in June. Your wife and daughter will probably be very sick, I'm afraid."

"I see," said Mr Haddock, and then he

[25]

added, by way of explanation, "Is there a collar button under your foot by any chance?"

"What kind?" asked Mr Sills, bending over and joining in the search.

"Spalding Red Dot," said Mr Haddock.

"I lost a Red Dot just about here on my last trip," said Mr Sills.

"Mine were marked H.N.Q." said Mr Haddock and then he added, apologetically, "My wife's initials. They were a wedding present."

"I find lately that I get more distance," said Mr Sills, "with a Wright and Ditson."

"Here it is," said Mr Haddock, and he triumphantly produced the little truant.

"Good," said Mr Sills, brushing off his knees. "You know they say that when they drain out these washrooms in the Fall the porters often find thirty-five and forty collar buttons."

"You were speaking about seasickness," said Mr Haddock.

"I'll tell you the only sure way to avoid

being sick," said Mr Sills, "and that is to eat a lot of fruit."

"Thank you," said Mr Haddock, "and thank you very much for helping me look for that button."

"Not at all, brother," said Mr Sills. "We all live in the world together."

"It would be a mighty funny place if we didn't," replied Mr Haddock.

"That's right, brother," said Mr Sills. "A mighty funny place. Live and learn and a strong pull together."

"And eat a lot of fruit," added Mr Haddock.

"Right, brother," said Mr Sills. "God's way is best and say, if you get to Genoa, look up——"

But Mr Haddock had gone.

Mr Haddock found Mrs Haddock and Mildred dressed and ready for breakfast.

"Good morning, dear," said Mr Haddock. "The porter says we are on time. Did you sleep well?"

"No," said Mrs Haddock.

"I did," said little Mildred.

Just then a railroad conductor came through the train.

"Are we on time, conductor?" asked Mr Haddock, addressing the conductor.

"Two hours late," replied the conductor.

"Thank you," said Mr Haddock. "And which direction is the dining car?"

"Forward," replied the conductor.

In the next car Mr Haddock stopped to ask the porter if they were on time.

"One hour late, suh," replied the porter.

"Thank you," said Mr Haddock.

In the next car they found a Pullman car conductor and Mr Haddock showed him his tickets.

"Are we on time?" asked Mr Haddock.

"Thirty minutes late," replied the Pullman car conductor.

"We're gaining," said Mr Haddock, and they moved on.

"Mildred," said Mrs Haddock. "You mustn't look in the berths as you go along."

"I have seen some very interesting things,"

said Mildred, "and have several questions to ask you."

"Later," suggested Mrs Haddock, feeling in her mother's heart that before breakfast was not the right time.

After passing through five more cars they reached the diner.

"Three," said Mr Haddock to the head waiter.

"Three," replied the head waiter, understanding instantly what was wanted.

"Are we on time?" asked Mr Haddock somewhat fearfully.

"Two and a half hours late," said the head waiter, pulling out his watch and three chairs.

"We must have just crossed the equator then," said Mr Haddock, mournfully looking out of the window.

"You lose a whole day when you go to China," said Mildred, "and I should like some syrup on my oatmeal."

"You can't have any syrup on your oatmeal," said Mr Haddock, but before Mildred had had time to cry, a stranger in a Palm

Beach suit had seated himself at their table and begun to pick his teeth.

"Mildred," exclaimed Mrs Haddock, and she stopped the child's hand just as it was reaching for the toothpick bowl.

"Why not?" asked the surprised child and, pointing to the stranger, she said, "He is."

In order to quickly change the subject before the stranger might become embarrassed, Mr Haddock turned to Mrs Haddock and said, "And is it really true that in the past forty-five years no American has ever been able to scale Mont Blanc?" and at the same time he gave Mildred a kick under the table, so that thanks to his quick wit the incident passed off practically unnoticed.

After Mr Haddock had eaten his griddle cakes, of which he was not particularly fond, the conversation became more general.

"So you're going to Europe?" said the stranger, probably a Mr Smith of Toledo.

"Yes," said Mr Haddock. "I thought I would take my wife and daughter over," and he indicated with his hand which was his wife and which his daughter.

"I've been across," said Mr Smith.

"Were you seasick going over?" asked Mrs Haddock quickly.

"Yes," said Mr Smith, "and coming back it was worse."

"Oh dear me," said Mrs Haddock, and she looked at her husband in distress.

"Possibly you are a poor sailor," suggested Mr Haddock.

"There are no poor sailors," said Mildred. "There are only good artists and bad artists."

"My daughter reads a lot," explained Mr Haddock. "She got that out of a book."

"Oh" said the stranger and he moved his chair a little away from the girl who was playing "fives" with her knife.

"I tell you what, though," said Mr Smith. "I've got a sure cure for seasickness."

"A gentleman I met a little while ago," said Mr Haddock, "told me to eat lots of fruit."

"Ah!" said Mr Smith. "Stay off of fruit. Don't touch fruit. Fruit causes more seasickness than all other causes," and he called for his check from the waiter.

"That's very interesting," said Mr Haddock.

"Let me put that in my note book," said Mrs Haddock and from her bag she drew out "My Trip Abroad."

"I'll have to put it under 'Places Visited and Interesting People Met'" she said to Mr Haddock. "I haven't any more room under 'Notes—Miscellaneous.'"

"That will be all right," said Mr Haddock magnanimously, so Mrs Haddock borrowed his pencil and wrote "Sea Sickness Cure—a gentleman in the dining car on the way to New York with a white-wash necktie says——" and then she looked at Mr Smith. "What did you say?"

"When?" he asked.

"Just now," she replied, "about sea sickness."

"Oh," replied Mr. Smith. "I said to eat no fruit and stay up on deck as much as possible.

[32]

It's staying in their cabins that makes people sea sick."

"Thank you very much," said Mrs Haddock, and she wrote it into the book. "STAY ON DECK—NO FRUIT."

"Not at all," said Mr Smith, and turning to the waiter he said, "Are we on time, chief?"

"I don't know," replied the waiter.

"What did you say?" asked Mr Haddock, doubting his ears.

"I said I didn't know whether we were on time or not," said the waiter.

"I would like to shake your hand," said Mr Haddock, "and this is my wife, Mrs Haddock, and my only daughter Mildred."

"Thank you, sir," said the waiter blushing. "I feel that I only did right in telling you the truth."

"What time is it, by the way?" asked Mr Smith.

"I have eight forty," said Mr Haddock, "but I forgot to turn my watch an hour forward for Eastern time."

"You mean backward, don't you, sir?" said the waiter.

"I don't know," said Mr Haddock.

"I think I can explain it to you, sir," said the waiter, and running hastily out to the kitchen he returned with an orange and a small oil lamp which he proceeded to light.

"Now this lamp," he said, "will be the sun. Would you mind holding it there, madam? Thank you, madam. And this orange," he continued, "is the earth. Now, as everybody knows, the earth revolves around the sun once a year, thus," and he moved the orange slowly around the lighted lamp which Mrs Haddock was carefully holding.

"But," went on the waiter, "the earth *also* revolves on its own axis, thus, and so we have day and night."

"That's right," said Mr Haddock, thoughtfully. "Day and night."

"Now," continued the waiter, "let us put a pin into this orange at a point representing the city in which you live. Have you a pin or two, sir?"

[34]

"Yes," said Mr Haddock, and he took two pins out of the lapel of his coat which he had been saving there for eight years for just some such purpose as this.

"Thank you, sir," said the waiter. "And we will let this gentleman put in this other pin at a point representing New York," whereupon Mr Smith carefully pushed in the other pin.

"Now," said the waiter, rolling up his sleeves, "observe closely. I pass the orange around the lamp. It is six o'clock in New York. What time is it where you live?"

"Five o'clock," said Mr Haddock, scratching his head.

"Exactly," said the waiter, "and so, when you come to New York, you turn your watches an hour backward. Thank you very much," and taking the lamp from Mr Haddock, he blew it out, took the orange, tossed it in the air, cut it in two, showed one half to Mr Haddock, one half to Mr Smith, and with a polite bow he brushed a few crumbs off the table and backed his way down the aisle.

"I saw how he did it," said Mildred. "He had another orange in his pocket."

Mr Smith had borrowed Mr Haddock's pencil and was figuring rapidly all over the back of the menu.

"He's wrong," he finally, but triumphantly, announced. "Look."

Mr and Mrs Haddock looked.

"There's your circumference of the earth," he said excitedly. "Multiply that by Pi or 3.1416, and what do you get?"

"I don't know" said Mr Haddock. "I took the classical course."

"You get X," said Mr Smith. "And dividing X by your known quantity gives you, in round figures, Greenwich Mean Time. Then all you have to do is point off and you get— WAITER!" he suddenly called, looking around in the direction in which the waiter had disappeared.

A waiter came out from the kitchen but he had a moustache.

"Are you our waiter?" asked Mr Smith.

"No sir," replied the man. "Your waiter

has gone off. Here is your check, sir," and he handed Mr Haddock the bill on a silver tray.

Mr Smith regarded the waiter fixedly, all the while chewing the end of Mr Haddock's pencil.

"I think that's a false moustache," he suddenly announced. "I think you are the same waiter."

The waiter started and drew back.

"Oh no, sir," he replied. "Not I, sir. I wouldn't do anything like that, sir. I have my wife and children to think of."

He pulled a photograph from his pocket and showed it to Mrs Haddock.

"That's my youngest, madam," he said. "She will be five next month."

"Well, well," said Mr Haddock, "quite a youngster."

"Do you know anything about mathematics?" demanded Mr Smith.

"Yes sir," replied the waiter, blushing.

"Look at that, then," said Mr Smith, and he showed him his menu filled with figures

[37]

which the waiter took and examined carefully for several seconds.

"You're wrong, sir," he finally announced. "You've forgotten to add Z, if I may say so, sir."

"What Z?" demanded Mr Smith cautiously.

"Daylight saving time," replied the waiter and with a smile he took his photograph and retired.

"I don't think we ought to have to pay for that orange," said Mrs Haddock looking at the bill.. "I really don't, Will. We didn't order it."

Mr. Smith was figuring very hard again but he glanced up.

"That orange is Dutch," he announced.

"Nonsense," said Mr Haddock. "I've got the change right here."

"No sir—it's Dutch," insisted Mr Smith.

"You can pay for the next one," said Mr Haddock.

Mr Smith had returned to his mathematics.

"Will you excuse us?" said Mr Haddock.

Mr and Mrs Haddock Abroad

Mr Smith did not look up from his figuring and the Haddock family arose as one man, and moved down the aisle.

"That orange is Dutch," said Mr Smith, reaching for another sheet of paper. "Absolutely Dutch," but the Haddocks were just going out of the door and did not hear him.

"Absolutely Dutch," murmured Mr Smith as he began to fill the back of another menu with figures and that was the last they ever saw of him or of Mr Haddock's pencil.

CHAPTER II

"New York!" called the conductor confidently, and it *was* New York, because the conductor had been with the road forty-two years.

"A taxi cab," said Mr Haddock to the Red Cap who grabbed his bag.

"I can carry this all right," said Mrs Haddock, drawing away.

"Nonsense, dear," said Mr Haddock. "Give him your bag. It's only a dime." So Mrs Haddock surrendered her bag to the nice patronizing negro.

"Do you really think we need to take a taxi cab?" she asked her husband.

"Certainly, dear," said Mr Haddock, who had been to New York before. "And which color would you choose?"

They walked along in silence for several minutes, and finally Mrs Haddock said:

"Pink."

"A pink taxi cab," said Mr Haddock to the porter.

"All out of pink," said the porter, and Mrs Haddock bit her lip in vexation.

"Well—lavender then," she finally said, "light lavender."

"All out of lavender," said the porter.

"Oh dear!" said Mrs Haddock.

"Black and white, black and white checker, yellow, yellow checker, green—hey Frank!" he called to a nearby cab starter.

"Wot?" replied Frank.

"Any more green?"

"Naw," replied Frank.

"No more green," said the Red Cap. "Hurry up, lady."

"Well, I'll take yellow—no—black and white—no—yellow," said Mrs Haddock. "But Will, don't you take it just because I did."

"No, I really wanted yellow," said Mr Haddock.

"Honestly?" asked Mrs Haddock.

[41]

Mr and Mrs Haddock Abroad

"Yes, honestly," said Mr Haddock, smiling at her reassuringly.

"A yellow for three," he said to the porter; "and the check, please—we're in a hurry."

By the time they had got into the cab all were smiling again and Mr Haddock insisted that he would ride backward on the little seat.

After they had sat there expectantly for some time without moving, the taxi driver leaned around, opened the door and said "Well where do youse want to go?"

"Oh," said Mr Haddock, "I forgot. Why —we want to go to a good hotel. Do you know the name of any?"

"I would say the Ritz," replied the taxi driver, "if I hadn't heard lately that the cuisine had fallen off a bit. There really aren't any good hotels in New York any more."

"Is it near Grant's Tomb?" asked Mrs Haddock. "I want to see Grant's Tomb this afternoon."

"How about the Waldorf?" asked Mr Haddock.

The taxi driver shrugged his shoulders.

"I'll take you there, of course, if you want to go," he said, "but——"

"Maybe that gentleman could help us," said Mr Haddock, indicating a white clad Street Cleaner who was busily plying his trade nearby.

"Oh Mr Perkins," called the taxi driver, and the Street Cleaner laid down his cigarette, stroked his moustache once or twice, and came up to the cab.

"Mr Perkins," said the taxi driver, "this is my friend Mr——"

"Haddock," said Mr Haddock; "and this is Mrs Haddock and my daughter Mildred."

"How do you do?" said Mr Perkins, removing his white hat and one white glove and bowing politely. "Not the Boston Haddocks?"

"No," said Mr Haddock. "We're from the middle west."

"Ah, yes," said Mr Perkins. "I see." And the tone of his voice became somewhat more reserved.

[43]

"My grandfather came from Boston though," asserted Mrs Haddock proudly.

"Of course," said Mr Perkins. "Of course. And this is your first visit to our city, Mr Haddock?"

"No indeed," said Mr Haddock quickly. "I have been here twice before—once for three days and once for two."

"Charming place, don't you think?" said Mr Perkins. "But probably you don't like it —most strangers don't at first. Mrs Perkins and I are very fond of New York—and it's really the best summer resort in America, too. We wouldn't go anywhere else for the world. Are you here for long, Mrs Haddock?"

"We sail for Europe to-morrow" said Mrs Haddock.

"Ah yes," said Mr Perkins. "On the Aquitania?"

"No," said Mr Haddock, after an embarrassing pause.

"We couldn't get passage," added Mrs Haddock quickly.

"I see," said Mr Perkins, stroking his moustache with a slight smile. "Well, well—I certainly envy you. Paris, I suppose?"

"Yes," said Mr Haddock.

"Ah—Paris, Paris," said Mr Perkins, and leaning on his broom handle he smiled reflectively. "I suppose Berry Wall and the Princesse de Lorme are still holding forth at Longchamps. You *must* go to Longchamps for the races."

"Are you fond of horses?" asked Mrs Haddock sympathetically.

"I detest horses," said Mr Perkins with a sudden convulsive grasp of his broom handle.

"Oh," said Mrs Haddock, biting her lip, "I'm so sorry. I forgot."

"Oh, not at all," said Mr Perkins, smiling again. "I beg of you. But you really must go to Longchamps for the Grand Prix—everybody will be there."

"We thought something of going to Rome, too," said Mrs Haddock.

"But my dear lady," said Mr Perkins, "nobody will be in Rome at this time of the year."

[45]

"We wanted to see the Coliseum," explained Mr Haddock.

"Ah yes," said Mr Perkins, "the tourist thing. Well, well—I certainly envy you Paris. Perhaps Mrs Perkins and I shall get over next year. It's almost impossible to get away this summer, though—there's the convention for one thing—you know what that means——"

"Yes, indeed," said Mrs Haddock, sympathetically.

"But perhaps, next year, business will let up a bit," said Mr Perkins.

"How is business?" asked Mr Haddock, offering Mr Perkins a cigar.

"Only fair" replied Mr Perkins. "I've got the Yale Club block this week." And Mr Perkins shrugged his shoulders. "But next week I hope to get Brooks Brothers—and in July, if I'm lucky, I'll get the Racquet Club —I've had my application in for a long time —or perhaps the Ritz."

"That's fine!" said Mr Haddock. "And that reminds me that we wanted to ask you

[46]

about hotels. You see, we are only here for the night."

"Well," said Mr Perkins, "the Ritz would do for one night."

"I'd heard," said the taxi driver, who had been an interested listener to all that had gone before, "that the cuisine had fallen off a bit."

"I doubt it," said Mr Perkins, lighting his cigar. "I doubt it for several reasons. But for that matter," he said, "you probably would want to dine out somewhere anyway."

"Yes," said Mr Haddock, "we would sort of like to see a little New York high life— Broadway, you know, and the gay White Way."

"Well, of course," said Mr Perkins, "we New Yorkers really don't know anything about that sort of thing, so I really can't help you there. But try the Ritz anyway—or the St. Regis—and I'm frightfully sorry but I see the Inspector coming and I've got to be running along to my job. Awfully nice. Good-bye."

[47]

"Glad to have met you," said Mrs Haddock, shaking his hand.

"I'm out in front of the Yale Club almost every day," said he to Mr Haddock. "Goodbye."

And tipping his hat and pulling on his gloves, he returned to his work just in time to give the Inspector a pleasant smile as he passed.

"A thoroughly nice fellow!" was Mr Haddock's comment, "and just the right man for the job."

Then he turned to the taxi driver and said "I think we'll take a chance on the Ritz."

"Very good, Sir," said the driver, and with that he reached over and pulled down his flag, for he had felt all along that it would have been unfair to Mr Haddock to have charged him for the time he had spent in the taxi cab while it was standing still.

Soon they were at the Ritz, where they were unable to obtain accommodations, so after going to four more hotels they at last found suitable quarters just above 40th street.

Mr and Mrs Haddock Abroad

I wish I might take the time to tell you of the many delightful experiences our three travellers had in the wonderful city of New York that afternoon and night, but this is, after all, an account of their trip to Europe, not to New York, and besides, as a matter of fact, they had a rotten time and were grossly overcharged for some terrible food, and Grant's Tomb was closed and Mrs Haddock went to sleep in the theatre and little Mildred got a bad oyster, so I shall save all that for some other time.

Bright and early the next morning they were awakened by the cheery sound of a little steam riveter busily running to and fro over an iron beam just outside their window and ever and anon chirping his merry song, "Can't see me. Can't see me. Here I am. Can't see me."

"This city is certainly being built up rapidly," said Mr Haddock. "It ought to be a pretty good real estate investment."

"Now dear," said Mrs Haddock, who had been up and dressed since five o'clock, "you promised me you weren't even going to think of business on this trip."

"All right," said Mr Haddock, "but what would you say to a little breakfast?"

"Do you think the dining room is open yet?" asked Mrs Haddock.

"Sure," replied Mr Haddock. "It's seven thirty. Come, Mildred!" for Mildred was trying to get razor blades, shaving soap, tooth paste, and a gauze bandage out of a machine in the bathroom.

"You have to put a quarter in to get anything," said her father.

"I think I can get it without that," said little Mildred, "if I only had a hammer and a cold chisel."

"The hammer is packed in the trunk," said her mother. "I didn't think we would need it until we got on the boat."

"I'll have one sent up," said Mr Haddock, who had been in hotels before, and with that he stepped to the telephone.

"Oh I wouldn't, dear," said Mrs Haddock. "We'll have to tip that boy again."

"Nonsense!" said Mr Haddock, and he moved the telephone "jigger" up and down vigorously for several minutes, at the same time saying "Hello hello hello hello hello hello hello hello hello" once or twice.

Finally someone answered by saying "H E L L O !"

"Oh," said Mr Haddock. "Excuse me. I didn't think anyone would hear me. I was just trying out a new telephone."

"What do you want?" asked the voice.

"I would like a hammer and a chisel——"

"A cold chisel," called Mildred from the bathroom.

"Yes, a hammer, a chisel, and some cracked ice in Room 476," said Mr Haddock.

"I'll give you the Bell Captain," said the voice.

"Oh goody!" said Mr Haddock. "She's going to give me the Bell Captain."

"I'm very proud of you," said Mrs Haddock simply.

"I owe everything to you, dear," was Mr Haddock's reply. "Everything."

A look of mutual understanding was in their eyes but at the end of nine minutes Mr Haddock said: "Dear, I'm afraid the Bell Captain is a Bell Captain in name only," and he sadly hung up.

"I'm getting very hungry," said Mrs Haddock. "Come, Mildred—some other time."

"Oh, shoot!" said Mildred, but she was a normal child as regards breakfast and so they went out, slamming the door after them.

"Have you got the key?" asked Mr Haddock while they were waiting for the elevator.

"Oh, dear!" said Mrs Haddock, "I left it on the dresser!"

"Down!" called Mr Haddock, but the elevator was going up and did not stop.

"We'll get it when it comes down," said Mr Haddock wisely, and they almost did.

"Down?" asked Mr Haddock of the neatly uniformed boy.

"Down," replied the boy.

"Down, then!" said Mr Haddock, and they started up.

"Oh dear!" exclaimed Mrs Haddock.

[52]

"It's just this car, ma'am," said the boy. "The brakes don't work very well."

"Oh dear!" exclaimed Mrs Haddock again.

"Maybe you're giving it too much gas," suggested Mr Haddock. "I sometimes have the same trouble with the Buick."

"It's a new car," explained the boy. "It's really a dealer's car. Mr Otis let us have it while ours was being overhauled." And so after they had gone three and a half floors up the car stopped and started down.

"Do you have much trouble in winter?" asked Mr Haddock.

"Not if we don't leave it out all night," replied the boy. "Sometimes it starts a little hard in the morning."

"I generally pour a little hot water on the carbureter," said Mr Haddock.

"That's very good," said the boy, "and alcohol is very good too."

"Isn't it!" said Mr Haddock with a reminiscent smile, and then he added, "This is Mrs Haddock and my daughter Mildred."

"How do you do?" said the elevator boy

cordially, but just then the elevator stopped and started upwards again.

"Oh for God's sake," said little Mildred fretfully, "let's get out of here. I'm hungry!"

"Hush dear," said her father, somewhat embarrassed and turning to the elevator boy he explained "She will be eleven next August."

"Indeed!" said the elevator boy, but it was five and a quarter floors before he could bring the car to a full stop.

"Are you interested in steamships?" asked Mrs Haddock, seeing that their host was becoming somewhat embarrassed by the way his elevator was behaving.

"Only in an amateur way," replied the boy. "I've read a great deal about steamships but I don't really think you can get much out of books, do you?"

"No," replied Mrs Haddock frankly. "I only happened to mention steamships because we are sailing for Europe this noon."

"I'm taking my wife and daughter across," added Mr Haddock in conversational tones.

"Isn't that jolly!" exclaimed the boy, and then he added "I've been over."

"Were you sick?" asked Mrs Haddock as the car slowly passed the fourth floor.

"Very!" said the boy.

"Oh dear!" said Mrs Haddock.

"I'll tell you, though," said the boy, "I've got a sure cure for sea sickness."

"Indeed," said Mrs Haddock, interested. "A gentleman we met a little while ago told us to be sure and walk on deck as much as possible."

"Ah!" exclaimed the boy, "that's the worst thing you could possibly do."

"Indeed!" said Mr Haddock.

"No Sir," said the boy emphatically. "Don't do that. Stay in your cabin all the time. Lie down in your cabin."

"What about fruit?" asked Mr Haddock.

"Fruit doesn't make any difference one way or the other," said the boy. "But stay in your cabin the first four days."

"Thank you very much!" said Mr Haddock.

[55]

"I must make a note of that," said Mrs Haddock.

"I'm not criticising," said Mr Haddock, "but wasn't that the main floor we just passed?"

"Yes," replied the boy, "but I couldn't get her to stop there. We'll surely stop at the cellar. You won't mind getting out there, will you?"

"Not at all," replied Mr Haddock, "and as a matter of fact I had an errand to do right near the cellar and you aren't taking us a bit out of our way."

"You're awfully nice to say so," said the boy.

"And probably you can get much better parking space down there," said Mrs Haddock.

"Oh, that wouldn't make any difference," said the boy, and with that the car came to a stop.

"Bully landing!" said Mr Haddock, and they got out into the cellar.

"I'm sorry," said the boy, "but I've got to

be running along. Can't drop you anywhere else, can I?"

"No, thanks," said Mr Haddock. "This is just right."

"Good bye!" said Mrs Haddock, and they waved their hands at him as he shot up out of sight.

"Watch, dear," said Mr Haddock, grabbing his wife's hand and pointing to the indicator over the elevator door. "He's already at the mezzanine—now the third—now the fifth—my God—he's down—no—he's up—he's passing the sixth—there he goes——"

"Oh I can't look—I can't look!" cried Mrs Haddock. "Suppose he shouldn't stop at the top! Mildred—shut your eyes!"

Feverish, with tense, taut faces, the three sat watching the young boy's wild ride with Death, for Death was riding in that car, Death the Great Prompter who has rung down the Final Curtain on many a hotel elevator.

"He's at the thirteenth!" whispered Mr

Haddock through clenched teeth and he shut his eyes as if in prayer.

And then from the floor above them came the sound of great cheering—of men gone crazy, of hysterical women—shrieks, horns, whistles—a veritable bedlam of noise let loose.

Mr Haddock opened his eyes and leaped to his feet. "Look, dear!" he cried. "Look! He's stopped! He's stopped! He stopped just above the top floor. Yeaaa!"

And too happy for words they got up and filed out of the cellar, leaving behind them only a few torn programs and some peanut shells and a derby or two as mute, silent witnesses of the thousands who had been there before.

CHAPTER III

"Is this the boat for Europe?" asked Mr Haddock of the uniformed attendant at the gang plank.

"No, sir," replied he. "The boat for Europe has left."

"Oh, dear!" said Mrs Haddock.

Mr Haddock's lips tightened and he grabbed his four suitcases and gave Mildred to the porter and strode over to another man in uniform.

"Is this the boat for Europe?" he asked.

"Yes, sir," replied he.

"This seems a little foolish," said Mr Haddock, wiping the perspiration from his forehead. "That man over there told me the boat for Europe had left."

"Aw, he doesn't know what he's talking about," said the man. "He's new on the job."

"Oh!" said Mr Haddock, and so he and

[59]

Mrs Haddock and little Mildred showed their tickets and their passports and walked over the gang plank into the floating palace that was to transport them to the land of their dreams.

"When does the bar open?" asked Mr Haddock of the steward who was carrying their bags to their stateroom.

"When we drop the pilot," replied the steward.

"Why, is he a prohibition agent?" asked Mrs Haddock, but the steward had already entered their stateroom.

"Here you are, sir," he said in English.

"Ah, yes," said Mr Haddock, and then he added, "Ah, yes."

"Electric lights," said the steward, snapping a switch and flooding the stateroom with artificial light. "Modern plumbing," and he pointed to what looked like a folding desk, "Hot and cold running water," and he pulled open the desk and revealed a wash basin with faucets.

"It would be a bit small to give very large

parties in," said Mr Haddock. "What do you think, dear?"

"Ah, but the location," said the steward, "right on the sea. Sea breezes every night. And the view!"

"That's something," said Mr Haddock.

"You can see Mount Monadnock on a clear day," said the steward.

"Really!" said Mrs Haddock.

"A beautiful neighborhood," said the steward. "How many children have you?"

"One," said Mr Haddock, pointing to Mildred. "And one married son. He's living with his wife, though," he added.

"I tell you what," said the steward confidentially. "You'd be making a great mistake not to take this."

"If we had any more children," said Mr Haddock to Mrs Haddock, "we could build."

"Exactly," said the steward. "Every man ought to own his own home."

"How about transportation?" asked Mr Haddock shrewdly.

[61]

The steward shrugged his shoulders. "The very best," he replied.

"What do you think, dear?" asked Mr Haddock.

"Well," said Mrs Haddock, "we could move that bunk over there—and put that wash-stand under the window."

"I'm sorry," said the steward, "but that wash-stand can't be moved."

"What direction is that?" asked Mrs Haddock, pointing out of the port hole.

"South," replied the steward.

"Hmmm—sun in the afternoon," said Mrs Haddock.

"I'll guarantee it," said the steward, "except under unfavorable weather conditions."

"Such as, for instance, clouds," said Mr Haddock.

"How about mosquitoes?" asked Mrs Haddock.

"You can look at me," said the steward, starting to remove his white coat. "I haven't been bitten all year."

"Well!" said Mrs Haddock, "we might try it, Will. After all, it *is* near the sea."

"The best thing in the world," said the steward to Mr Haddock, "for hay fever."

"But I haven't got hay fever," said Mr Haddock.

"Are you sure?" asked the steward, and Mr Haddock felt very uncomfortable.

"How do you like it, Mildred?" said Mrs Haddock.

"I'm sure the little girl will like it," said the steward quickly, giving Mildred a nice smile. "All children do."

"Oh, they do, do they?" said Mildred.

"Yes, they do, do they," said the steward, and he added, "What a disagreeable child!"

"Isn't she," agreed Mr Haddock. "And we have tried so hard, too."

Just then a loud blast of a whistle sounded from above.

"Oh, dear!" said Mrs Haddock, "we're near a factory. That means a lot of smoke and soot, Will."

"Not at all, madam," said the steward,

"that's just the boat signalling. We'll be leaving in ten minutes now."

"Let's go upstairs," said Mr Haddock, "and see us leave. And, steward, just put those bags under the bunk."

"Yes, sir," said the steward, and as they were leaving he aimed a sly kick at Mildred but missed.

Upstairs, on the main deck, all was bustle and confusion.

"Everybody off!" yelled a tall man in a blue uniform, blowing a shrill whistle. "Everybody off!"

"That doesn't mean us," said Mr Haddock, clutching his wife's arm. "I'm sure it doesn't, dear."

So they stayed on, and after a while people began running down gangplanks, blowing whistles, and running up gangplanks with baskets of fruit and flowers, and on the shore people began waving handkerchiefs and American flags, and calling "Goodbye," and on the boat people began throwing kisses and flowers, and Ganna Walska began to be pho-

tographed for the Sunday supplements, and
tugs began whistling in the river, and an air-
plane flew past overhead and the man next to
Mr Haddock began trying to tell somebody
on shore that he had forgot to telephone Mrs
McDonald about the something fixtures, and
the man on shore wasn't getting it very well,
and "I guess we're off," said Mr Haddock,
and it was so exciting that his voice broke a
little and Mrs Haddock began to cry.

And half an hour later he looked at his
watch and said, "I wonder why we don't
start."

And an hour later the people on the dock
began to feel a little foolish, and the people
on the boat began to feel a little irritated, and
some of them went below to their staterooms,
and some of the people on the dock went
home, and then finally the ship's whistle blew
another big long blast, and they let down the
gangplank, and on walked Mayor Hylan's
son-in-law, and they started.

"Well, I guess we're off," said Mr Haddock
with just the shadow of a doubt in his voice,

[65]

but as the boat swung around into the river and moved down past the Woolworth building and the Battery, his doubts gradually became a little dissipated.

"There's the Statue of Liberty," whispered Mrs Haddock, who was really very excited.

"Look, Mildred!" said Mr Haddock, "there's the Statue of Liberty."

"I'm hungry," said Mildred, and so he knew they were really off for Europe.

When they went down to their stateroom to wash for lunch they were surprised and delighted to find seven baskets and eleven boxes, containing among other things 103 oranges, 67 bunches of hot-house grapes, 241 fresh figs, 119 cured figs, and 141 prunes.

"This one is from Mrs Gueminder," said Mrs Haddock, reading a card.

"I wonder how she knew I was so constipated," mused Mr Haddock, but delighted, just the same, with the timely gift.

Mrs Haddock began folding up the tissue paper and string in order to save them for some occasion in their travels when they might be terribly in need of tissue paper and string, while Mr Haddock took out a pencil and began figuring on the back of an envelope.

"Dear," he said at last, "I may be a fraction of a decimal off, either plus or minus, but in round numbers I figure that if we concentrate all our efforts and cut out theaters and sleep we can just finish the last of this fruit before we get to France."

"Oh, dear!" said Mrs Haddock, "what *will* we do with it all?"

"Eat it!" said Mr Haddock. "Now, for the first three days I have allotted you 165 grapes, 68 figs, 54 prunes, and 49 oranges."

"But I don't like oranges," said Mrs Haddock.

"That doesn't matter," said Mr Haddock severely. "In a crisis like this we must forget our petty individual likes or dislikes and work only for the good of the whole."

"Our forefathers" — and Mr Haddock pointed to the large American flag above him —"who wisely forged this country out of the melting pot of European chaos—our fore-

[67]

fathers who beat their swords into plough-
shares in order that our children might today
enjoy the advantages of this beautiful new
free public school—the man whom we meet
today to honor and who gave his acres and his
name to this beautiful amusement park—
would not permit it. No, my friends," said
Mr Haddock, and the vast stateroom became
strangely hushed and quiet. "No, my friends,
the monument which we consecrate today
may be to some a mere drinking fountain in
the center of our beautiful city, where horses
may quench their thirst with water from our
proud Muscatawney and pass on, with, perhaps, a prayer of gratitude to the brave
little lady whose name it bears, but, my
friends——" And Mr Haddock's voice fell
impressively "to others, 'something more.'
There is another thirst, my friends—a higher
thirst—a more divine thirst. And in present-
ing to this convention this afternoon the name
of Alexander P. Sturgis I can only say that
he combines in one man all those qualities
which have so endeared him to rich and poor

alike and I point with pride—I point with pride, my friends— to the fact that he stands in a larger sense—in a larger sense——"

Mr Haddock stopped and wiped his brow nervously.

"In a larger sense," he repeated.

"Oh, dear!" whispered Mrs Haddock to Mildred. "That's just the place where he got stuck this morning."

"In a larger sense," said Mr Haddock, and someone tittered audibly. "In a larger sense," and then to everyone's intense relief he went on. "In a larger sense we cannot consecrate, we cannot dedicate, we cannot hallow this ground. The brave men living and dead who fought here have done so far beyond our petty power to add or detract. It is for us the living rather to consecrate our lives to the end that the ideals for which they fought shall not be forgotten and that government of the people, by the people, and for the people shall not perish from the earth. My friends, I thank you," and he put on his silk hat and sat down beside Mrs Haddock.

[69]

"You did awfully well, dear," she whispered behind her white gloved hand, but Mr Haddock was standing up and bowing and waving his hands to friends and suddenly he picked little Mildred up in his arms and let the crowd see her and the cheering grew louder than ever and then he made Mrs Haddock stand up and the crowd went wild and there was no doubt that if a vote had been taken then he would have been elected by a large plurality over Jones (Dem.) who had, however, made heavy gains upstate, especially among a certain discontented element in the cities and among the farmers in the rural districts where the new tariff hit hardest.

But just then a knock came on the door and a pink, chubby face appeared and said, "I'm the bath steward—and I'm afraid I'm awfully late."

"Not at all," said Mr Haddock. "Do come in. You know Mrs Haddock, of course—and this is Mildred, our youngest."

"Don't tell me this is Mildred," said the bath steward, patting the child's head. "Why, the last time I saw this little girl she was no bigger than a minute. Well, they do grow up, don't they."

"Don't they," said Mildred, drawing away from under his hand and quitting the state-room with an ill-concealed oath.

"I got caught in the traffic," explained the bath steward, "and I'm on my way to the Hemingways and I can just stay a minute."

"Awfully good of you to drop in," said Mrs Haddock. "Won't you have some fruit."

"Oh, don't bother, please," said the bath steward, taking a banana.

"It will just take a minute," said Mrs Haddock.

"Let her fix you some," said Mr Haddock. "She likes to do it, really."

"Oh, no, I couldn't think of it," said the bath steward, putting two oranges in his pocket. "I've really just finished lunch. At the Osborne's, you know—and what a lunch. Everybody was there. I'm surprised you weren't asked."

"The Osbornes don't seem to know us," said

Mrs Haddock. "I guess we don't move high enough for them. I met them once when he and Will were on that Booster committee together—you remember, Will, that afternoon at the Elks Club, and I will say that I never saw three such ill-behaved children in my life."

"Perfectly frightful!" said the bath steward, smiling sympathetically.

"They do say she has a lovely house," said Mrs Haddock. "But I certainly will not be the first to call, would you?"

"No, indeed!" murmured the bath steward.

"And I hear," went on Mrs Haddock, beginning to rock the boat back and forth with her chair, "that he and she have been on the verge of a divorce several times."

"I could tell you a lot worse than that," said the bath steward.

"Please sit down," said Mrs Haddock; "I don't think you find that bunk very comfortable. Will, you get up and give him that place and Mildred you run out again for a while, will you, dear?"

"No, really," said the bath steward, "I can't stay. I only dropped in to ask you what hour you wanted to take your bath."

"Awfully good of you," murmured Mr Haddock. "Please take some more fruit."

"What hours have you?" asked Mrs Haddock in a sudden businesslike manner.

"Well," said the bath steward, "of course, there has been quite a demand for hours this year."

"Of course," said Mr Haddock sympathetically.

"But I saved something very special for you and Mrs Haddock—one of our finest hours. Oh, I'm sure you'll be crazy about it."

"I'm sure we will," said Mr Haddock. "Can we take it with us now?"

"I think we had better see it first," said Mrs Haddock, practically.

"Why Hattie," said Mr Haddock, "do you think that's necessary? The gentleman has been so nice as to save it for us."

"I think we had better see it first," repeated Mrs Haddock, with dignity.

"Of course, madam," said the bath steward, and smiling understandingly at Mr Haddock, who felt quite a little embarrassed, he bowed his way out of the stateroom in order to get his bath book.

"You're such a fool, Will," said Mrs Haddock after he had gone, but before Mr Haddock had time to reply they were interrupted by the loud blast of a bugle blown just outside their door.

"Come in," said Mr Haddock, and he added reassuringly to his wife, "It's probably only a few soldiers. Don't bother to change your clothes."

But the bugle blew again and no one entered, so Mr and Mrs Haddock began reading the instructions regarding life belts.

"It's a little confusing," said Mr Haddock. "In the first place, that man in the picture has got a mustache——"

"You silly," said Mrs Haddock for the second time that day, "you don't have to have a mustache to wear a life belt properly."

"Are you sure?" asked Mr Haddock, but

[74]

just at that moment little Mildred burst into the cabin.

"That's the bugle for lunch," she announced, so with a few reassuring prunes and a cheery "Good luck" all around they went out into the corridor and down into the main dining saloon where they partook of luncheon in company with three other people who seemed to Mrs Haddock, as the meal progressed, to be a little strange.

"I think they are a little strange," she said to Mr Haddock after lunch, as they were sitting in their stateroom.

"What do you mean?" asked Mr Haddock.

"Well—that lady with the beard, for instance," said Mrs Haddock.

"What's wrong about that?" asked Mr Haddock, indignantly.

"Well, nothing," said Mrs Haddock baffled, "except that it is sort of funny to see her sitting there with a beard."

"My dear Harriet," said Mr Haddock, "you must remember that we are, after all, strangers here—practically guests of this boat.

And, furthermore, we are from the middle West and have had practically no contact with European life. So please, my dear Harriet," he said patiently, "let's try and not be too provincial."

"All right," said Mrs Haddock. "But I don't see why you have to make a fool of yourself over the first young chippet who comes along with a beard."

"I wasn't making a fool of myself," said Mr Haddock, somewhat exasperated. "I was just being nice to a young girl who seemed to be traveling alone."

"Alone!" said Mrs Haddock. "I'll bet she's alone! Who were those other two men?"

"I'm sure I don't know," said Mr Haddock. "Probably two international crooks."

"She spoke to them," said Mrs Haddock.

"On a boat like this," said Mr Haddock, "we are just one big family."

"There never was a bearded lady in our family," said Mrs Haddock, "and you know it."

[76]

"I assure you," said Mr. Haddock, jesting, "that my interests were purely tonsorial."

"Fiddlesticks," said Mrs Haddock. "Have some fruit?"

"No thank you," said Mr Haddock, putting his hands quickly in his pockets. "I'm not eating fruit. I think I shall go up on deck and walk."

"I shall lie here," said Mrs Haddock, "and eat fruit."

"One of you," said little Mildred, "is going to be very sea-sick before long and then I shall know which to do. I wish you would hurry, though, for I feel rather strange."

"Come with me, Mildred," said her father, but just then a knock came on the door and the steward appeared with some telegrams and letters.

"Haddock?" he asked.

"Haddock," replied Mr Haddock, for it was he.

"How do you spell it?" asked the steward, looking at the telegrams.

Mr and Mrs Haddock Abroad

"'H' as in 'Haddock,'" began Mr Haddock. "'A' as in 'Arthur'———"

"Arthur who?" asked the steward.

"I don't know," said Mr. Haddock.

"Nothing here for Arthur Haddock," said the steward.

"But that isn't my name," said Mr Haddock.

"What is your name?" asked the steward.

"Haddock," replied Mr Haddock, becoming a little exasperated. "William P. Haddock—and this is my wife———"

"Your wife?" asked the steward.

"My wife—my wife," screamed Mr Haddock. "Wife as in 'Wife taking my fun where I found it.'"

"Oh," said the steward. "Mrs Haddock."

"Practically," said Mr Haddock, "and that is my daughter Mildred. I'm sorry I lost my temper."

"I guess there's nothing for you," said the steward. "No—nothing for Mildred Haddock. Sorry."

[78]

"Well, is there anything for me?" asked Mr Haddock.

"I'll look," said the steward, and he looked.

"Is that you?" he said, and handed Mr Haddock a telegram.

"Yes," said Mr Haddock.

"That's all," said the steward, and he left, only to reappear almost immediately.

"Say, do you know a Mr —a Mr," and he looked at the letter, "a Mr Blumenstein—Mr Sol Blumenstein—I think that's it."

"No," replied Mr Haddock. "Sorry."

"Do you?" the steward then asked Mrs Haddock.

"No, I do not," she replied.

"Maybe you do?" he said, turning to Mildred.

"No," replied Mildred with a sneer. "I have not had the pleasure of Mr Blumenstein's acquaintance."

"He's a peach of a fellow," said the steward. "Well, good day."

"Good day," they called, cheerfully, and Mr Haddock opened the telegram.

"It's from Frank and Edith," he said.

"What does it say?" asked Mrs Haddock excitedly.

"Bon voyage," replied Mr Haddock.

"That means 'a good voyage' in French," said Mildred.

"How I envy you your knowledge of the language," said her father, but just then another knock came on the door and a passenger appeared.

"Mr Haddock?" he asked

"I think so," said Mr Haddock.

"Here are some letters and telegrams for you," the stranger said. "The steward just left them in my cabin. I opened them by mistake."

"Anything interesting?" asked Mr Haddock.

"No," said the stranger. "Not much. They all send much love and say 'have a good time.' Your Uncle George's teeth are worse—but then," and he smiled, "you know how Uncle George is."

"I'm surprised he's hung on this long," said Mr Haddock.

"Why doesn't he go to a good dentist?" asked the stranger.

"You've got me there," said Mr Haddock. "He's a bit 'near', you know."

"Anything else?" asked Mrs Haddock. "How were the twins?"

"Bully," said the stranger. "And oh yes—Alice Kent is going to have a baby in September."

"You don't say so," exclaimed Mr Haddock. "Well, well. What do you think of that, Hattie?"

"We'll be back by September," said Mrs Haddock. "Won't we now, Will?"

"Oh sure," replied her husband. "Anything else?"

"Well," said the stranger, "your Aunt Flora got into trouble with the gas company again the day you left and they've threatened to sue her—but I think it will be all right."

"Oh sure," said Mr Haddock. "Don't you

worry yourself about that. Well, it's mighty nice of you to bring these letters to us."

"Not at all," said the stranger. "Maybe you can do the same for me sometime."

"I'd be glad to," said Mr Haddock, and they shook hands and the stranger left.

"Here's a telegram he didn't open," said Mrs Haddock. "It's from Mame."

"What does she say?" asked Mr Haddock.

" 'Bon voyage,' " replied Mrs Haddock.

"That means 'a good voyage' in French," said Mr Haddock, chucking his daughter under the chin. "Come on, Mildred—let's go on deck."

On deck they found a number of people seated in steamer chairs.

"I wonder how one goes about getting a steamer chair," said Mr Haddock half to himself, half aloud, and there was a flash of smoke, a smell of sulphur, and a gentleman appeared, on whose face was a curiously sinister smile.

"I am the deck steward," he said.

"Oh yes," said Mr Haddock, a little nervously. "I want three chairs, about the center——"

The deck steward's smile became somewhat patronizing.

"The center has been sold out for the next eight weeks," he said wearily.

"Well—the side then," said Mr Haddock.

Just then a rather stout woman pushed her way between Mr Haddock and the deck steward and demanded, "Have you got something for Smithers?"

"But madam," protested Mr Haddock, and she turned and glared at him.

"What name?" asked the deck steward.

"Smithers—Mrs Pearl Smithers," she replied.

The deck steward consulted his book.

"Nothing here for Smithers," he said.

"Are you sure?" she demanded.

"Nothing for Smithers," said the deck steward. "Next."

"I want three chairs—" began Mr Haddock.

"But Mr Henderson said they would be left here in my name," continued Mrs Smithers.

"Nothing for Smithers, madam," said the deck steward.

"That's very funny," said Mrs Smithers.

"Next," said the deck steward.

"I'm sure Mr Henderson wouldn't have made a mistake," said the lady, turning to Mr Haddock.

"I'm sure he wouldn't," agreed Mr Haddock.

"Next," called the deck steward.

"Look under Talcott, then," said the woman. "H. A. Talcott."

"Nothing under Talcott, madam," said the deck steward.

"Firestone?" she suggested. "Mr or Mrs Firestone?"

"Nothing under Firestone," said the deck steward. "Please madam—*next!*"

"I would like three chairs—" began Mr Haddock automatically, but curiously enough he now found that he was third in line, two very large women having in some way gotten in ahead of him.

"What have you got in medium priced chairs?" asked the first lady.

"What night?" asked the deck steward.

The lady turned to the lady behind her.

"What night, Alice?" she asked.

"I don't know," said Alice. "How would Wednesday do?"

"Wednesday?" said the lady. "No—Wednesday the Freemans are coming to dinner."

"Please, madam," said the deck steward, "what night?"

"Thursday I can't get off," said Alice, "how about Tuesday?"

"All right," said the lady. "Tuesday," and she turned to the deck steward, "What have you got in medium priced chairs for Tuesday?"

"How many, madam?" he asked.

She turned to Alice.

"How many, Alice?" she asked.

"I don't know," said Alice. "Do you think Frank can come?"

"Oh, I wouldn't ask Frank," said the lady.

"Who would you ask?" asked Alice. "George?"

"How many, how many, how many?" said the deck steward.

By this time a rather long line had formed behind Mr Haddock, and signs of no small impatience were beginning to be manifested by the crowd.

"Well," said the lady, "we could get four and then if George couldn't come we could ask Frank."

"Or we could turn in the seat," suggested Alice.

"Can you turn in seats you don't use?" asked the lady of the deck steward.

"No, madam," he replied.

"Why not?" she asked.

"It's a rule of the management," said the deck steward. "How many seats do you want?"

"Well—four then," she replied.

"Four for Tuesday," he said. "Four on the side—second row."

Mr and Mrs Haddock Abroad

"How much?" she asked.

"Two twenty apiece with tax," he replied.

"How much?" she asked.

"Two twenty apiece," he repeated. "Please hurry, madam."

The lady turned to Alice.

"They're two twenty apiece," she said. "What do you think?"

Alice shook her head.

"Haven't you anything cheaper?" the lady asked.

"Not for Tuesday night," he replied.

Alice nudged her friend. "Ask about matinées," she said.

"When are matinées?" she asked.

"All sold out," he said.

"What?" asked the lady.

"All sold out," he repeated.

"Matinées? No more seats?" she asked.

"Matinées," he said, "all sold out."

"Oh shoot," said the lady. "What will we do, Alice?"

"I don't know," said Alice.

By this time the line behind Mr Haddock

and the two ladies had extended half way around the boat and out into the street and included men and women from all walks of life, for it did not seem that Alice and her friend were ever going to be able to decide what to do.

"It looks 'like rain," said Mr Haddock, stroking his long white beard and speaking not as one of them but as a prophet.

And it grew dark and in the distance could be heard rumblings of distant thunder.

"If there is a god," said Mr Haddock, who had been reading H. G. Wells only that morning, "and I strongly suspect that there is one— He will give us a sign."

And it grew darker and darker, and over the sea advanced the pattering rain, and storm clouds gathered over the plunging ship, and the wind whistled through the rigging, and then suddenly there was a terrific flash of lightning and a deafening peal of thunder, and then, out on the water, floated a large white object, too large to be a swan.

"A whale!" cried Mr Haddock, joyously.

"A miracle!" they all cried. "A miracle."

A CHOIR OF 300 MIXED VOICES FROM THE SOUTH BETHLEHEM TONKUNST
AND LIEDERKRANZ SOCIETY BURST INTO CHORUS—AND THE WHALE WAS
SLOWLY LIFTED OUT OF THE OCEAN.

Mr and Mrs Haddock Abroad

So they took Alice and her friend and threw them into the ocean, and the whale swallowed them, and a choir of 300 mixed voices from the South Bethlehem Tonkunst and Lieder-kranz Society burst into the final chorus, "Gott ist ewig," and the whale was slowly lifted out of the ocean and gradually but jerkily ascended into heaven with a slight creaking of ropes, and the afternoon was over.

"How did you like it?" asked Mr Haddock of an elderly gentleman as they slowly filed out.

The old gentleman shook his head sadly. "There aren't any good whales any more," he said. "Did you ever go to Bayreuth?"

"No," replied Mr Haddock.

"Ah me," sighed the old gentleman. "There were whales in those days."

"I bet there were," said Mr Haddock, who, under the broadening influence of this trip, was gradually becoming quite a bit of a philosopher. "I bet there were."

CHAPTER IV

"Land!" cried an excited sailor late that afternoon.

"You're crazy," replied the captain, "we've just started."

"My mistake," said the sailor, saluting, but under his breath he muttered, "I'll bet there was land there once."

"My, but you gave me a start," said the captain, and he took off his shoes again and the incident was forgotten.

It was true that they had comparatively just started, but as far as the eye could reach were vast expanses of water.

"It's like a veritable ocean," said the lady who occupied the deck chair next to Mr Haddock.

"It is indeed," replied Mr Haddock, reaching over to tuck Mrs Haddock's steamer blanket more closely about her.

Mr and Mrs Haddock Abroad

Mrs Haddock was sound asleep and Mr Haddock leaned back in his comfortable deck chair and closed his eyes happily.

It was nice to be sitting there and going to Europe with his wife and daughter. In five days practically they would be in Paris. Mr Haddock wondered what Paris was like. He picked up one of the guide-books which Mrs Haddock had brought along, and began to read.

"The breast stroke is negotiated more simply than the trudgeon or crawl," he read. "In the breast, or 'English' stroke, the beginner lies flat upon his or her stomach and at the count of one draws the legs sharply up to the position marked 'One' in the diagram."

Mr Haddock looked carefully at the diagram. "I wonder when they get to Paris," he remarked, and turned ahead several pages to see if by any chance there was a chapter coming soon headed "In Paris." But finding none, he returned to the text.

"At the count of 'Two,' " he read, "the beginner fills his or her lungs with air and kicks out convulsively——"

"Ouch!" yelled the lady next to Mr Haddock.

"Oh, I beg your pardon," said Mr Haddock apologetically. "I must have kicked you. Where does it hurt? Show Mr Haddock." So the lady pulled up her skirts.

"Does that hurt?" asked Mr Haddock, poking a spot in the calf of her left leg.

"No," said the lady. "And last Thursday those headaches came back."

"Hmmm," said Mr Haddock. "There?" with another poke a little higher up.

"No," said the lady.

"There?"

"No."

"William Haddock," said Mrs Haddock, waking up, "what are you doing?"

"Nothing," said Mr Haddock. "Honestly."

"William Haddock," said Mrs Haddock, "look at me."

"Honest," said Mr Haddock, "I was just

[94]

sitting next to this lady and my foot slipped and I kicked her."

"Is that all?" asked Mrs Haddock.

"Yes'm," said Mr Haddock, "you can ask her."

"William," said Mrs Haddock, "people don't kick strange ladies without some reason."

Just then the lady, who had returned to her reading and writing, looked up and frowned.

"Can you tell me," she asked, "an American Methodist minister who later became a well known pope?"

Mr Haddock scratched his head and began looking through his pockets.

"I had it written down somewhere," he said, "on the back of an envelope."

"You'd lose your head, Will," said Mrs Haddock sarcastically, "if it wasn't fastened on."

"It must be in two letters," said the lady, and she added, noticing Mrs Haddock for the first time, "It's a cross-word puzzle and I'm stuck."

Mr and Mrs Haddock Abroad

"Two letters?" said Mr. Haddock. "Try 'Ab.'"

"No," said the lady, "the first letter must be 'O' and the second one 'P.'"

"Op," said Mr Haddock. "That's it. Frank J. Op," and noticing his daughter playing with some other children at the opposite end of the deck he called, "Mildred."

"What?" yelled back the child.

"What were Frank J. Op's dates?" shrieked her father.

"1842-1899," yelled Mildred, "inclusive."

"Thanks," he screamed, and turning to the lady he said, "My daughter reads a great deal."

"Oh, you're a duck," said the lady, "and what is a kind of titmouse in five letters?"

"Meadow lark," suggested Mrs Haddock, and then she blushed and said, timidly, "I'm afraid I'm not much good at it."

"No, you're not," said the lady, somewhat frankly.

"Mrs Haddock plays a very good hand of whist," said Mr Haddock loyally.

"Why, Will," exclaimed Mrs Haddock, "whatever makes you say that? You know I can't," and turning to the lady she added, "I never was any good at games at-all."

"She can wiggle her ears," said Mr Haddock. "Go on, Hattie."

"Oh, there isn't room here," said Mrs Haddock, with a little giggle.

"Oh, please do," entreated the lady, so Mrs Haddock sat up very straight and wiggled her ears.

"Now, just the left one," said Mr Haddock proudly.

"Oh no, Will," said Mrs Haddock, "everybody's seen that so often."

"Oh, I haven't really," said the lady. "Oh, please do," so Mrs Haddock wiggled just the left one.

"That was the way Mrs Haddock and I became acquainted," said Mr Haddock, "She really can do it much better than that—you ought to see her when she's in practice."

"I should love to," said the lady, "she did it beautifully I thought."

"Oh, she can do much better than that," insisted Mr Haddock. "Can't you, Hattie?" and he patted his wife affectionately on the back while she smiled happily down at him.

"Will you have bouillon or tea?" asked the deck steward, suddenly appearing with a large tray full of cups and sandwiches.

"Bouillon," said the lady, and Mrs Haddock said "Bouillon," so the steward handed them two empty cups.

"I think I'll take tea," said Mr Haddock, who disliked tea very much, but he, too, received an empty cup.

"Delicious tea," said Mr Haddock, wiping his mouth with a mimic blue and white silk handkerchief.

"You're joking, Will," said Mrs Haddock, and turning to the lady she said, "My husband's such a joker at times."

But luckily, another steward soon appeared, followed by fifteen or sixteen small children, and this steward carried a tray on which were not only pots of tea and bouillon, but also many different kinds of sandwiches and cakes,

Mr and Mrs Haddock Abroad

and soon all were once more happily engaged in the process of digestion.

"Are you going to Paris first?" asked the lady.

"Yes," replied Mr Haddock, in the affirmative.

"Do you know Paris?" asked the lady.

"Only by reputation," said Mr Haddock. "I was trying to find out something about it only just now in one of those guide books, but I didn't seem to get very far," and he picked up the book and showed it to the lady.

"Oh, that's my swimming book," said the lady.

"Oh," said Mr Haddock, "I thought it seemed rather different from the ordinary guide book."

"You see," explained the lady, "I don't know how to swim."

"Mrs Haddock can swim," said Mr Haddock, "and dive."

"I have to hold my nose," said Mrs Haddock, modestly.

"Well, anyway," said the lady, "I thought that if anything happened to the boat it would be well to know something about swimming— at least to know what the different terms meant."

"You're quite right," said Mr Haddock, "and if we have any accidents I hope you will let me borrow it."

"Oh dear," said Mrs Haddock, "do you suppose anything *will* happen?"

Just then came the cry of "Captain overboard!" and the great powerful engines in the heart of the ocean greyhound momentarily stopped their ceaseless throbbing, while the appropriate flag meaning "Captain Overboard!" was hoisted to the peak and the passengers and the crew rushed to the rail of the boat, and hastily tossed over several life preservers marked "Captain Only!"

"There he is," shouted Mr Haddock, pointing to a head bobbing up and down in the water.

"Don't point, dear," said Mrs Haddock, patiently.

"Are you sure?" asked the lady.

"What does he look like?" asked Mr Haddock.

"He's very tall," said the lady.

"Yes," shouted Mr Haddock. "That's he."

"It's very rough," said the lady. "I'm afraid they'll have to go after him in a boat."

And sure enough, as soon as the crew had had time to change into the appropriate costume, a small tug filled with sailors, reporters, and a representative of the Chamber of Commerce, put out from the side of the ship.

"I did it on purpose," were the captain's first words, as they hauled him in over the side of the boat, "and I'm glad I did it. He was a beast."

"What do you think of conditions in Europe?" he was asked.

"Germany must pay," he replied, "but first of all France must disarm. England must destroy her battleships. Italy must give up her standing army. That's my solution."

"And how do you like New York?"

"A wonderful city," was the captain's reply.

"Such strength, such youth. Those buildings!
My! But ah—the noise! I was deafened.
And the hurry. Everyone is in such a hurry.
And those terrible—what do you call them?"

"Subways," was suggested.

"Yes—the subways. But I love New York
and hope to return there next year."

By this time the captain had reached his
vessel, where he stopped only long enough to
receive the keys of the ship from a little girl
representing "Neptune" and a little boy representing "Ireland," and to make a short
speech saying that he was glad that cordial
relations between the two great English speaking countries were yearly becoming more and
more closely cemented, and then, after being
photographed between the tallest and the
shortest sailor, he retired to his cabin to rest
for the night.

By this time it was six thirty or seven in the
evening, so that the sea was becoming quite a
bit rougher and they called Mildred and
started below.

"It makes you feel sort of funny, doesn't

it?" said Mr Haddock, as they walked rather unsteadily down the stairs toward the stateroom.

"Not yet," said Mrs Haddock, without too much confidence, "but perhaps you had better go up and walk on the deck some more."

"Oh, I didn't mean *that*," said Mr Haddock, "I meant that it was funny that here it is supper time with us and out home it is still only afternoon."

"Is it supper time?" asked Mrs Haddock.

"I hope so," said Mr Haddock. "This sea air certainly makes you feel hungry."

"I don't know, Will," said Mrs Haddock, "whether I want any supper or not."

"Ho, Ho, Ho," laughed Mr Haddock. "Don't tell me that *that* little amount of sea is affecting you. Why, I never felt better in my life," and he burst into a rousing sea chanty ending with several "Yo Ho Ho's" and a hearty slap in the middle of Mrs Haddock's back.

Mrs Haddock gave him a queer look which might have been interpreted to mean almost anything, but which really meant, "You just wait, you god damned fool," and they went into the stateroom.

"Well, Mildred," said Mr Haddock briskly, "do you enjoy going to Europe?"

"It's nice not to have to practice that old piano," replied the child, and then she added, "I ate fourteen sandwiches and that other boy only ate eleven, but I don't feel very well now."

"Well, well, well," said Mr Haddock, "your mother doesn't feel very well either. I'm afraid you two are not very good sailors." And with that he burst once more into a hearty song and poured the soapy water from his wash-basin into the drain with a nice sloshing noise.

"Don't do that Will, please," said Mrs Haddock from her bunk. "And Mildred, you come lie down beside Mother."

Just then the second bugle for dinner blew and Mr Haddock, whistling merrily, hastily brushed his hair and pulled on his coat.

"Better come along," he urged, "a good

meal will do you good." But as there was no response he chuckled slightly to himself and started for the door.

As he opened it the ship gave a tremendous lurch, followed by a slow deep plunge.

"Woops my dear," said Mr Haddock, bracing himself. "There she blows. Come on, old boy, let's see what you've got!" and full of confidence he closed the door of the stateroom and went towards the dining room.

After a while Mrs Haddock began to feel a little better.

"How do *you* feel, dear," she asked Mildred.

"Oh, much better," replied Mildred, getting up and reaching for some fruit.

Just then a low moan was heard on the corridor outside, the door opened slowly, and a pale, wan face appeared.

"Will!" exclaimed Mrs Haddock, sitting up.

"Haw, Haw," cried Mildred, pointing with delight, "it's the Ancient Mariner."

[105]

"Don't laugh, Mildred," said Mrs Haddock.

"I just thought," said Mr Haddock weakly, "that I would come down and see how you were getting along."

"We were just thinking," said Mildred, "of coming up and joining you in the dining room. Dinner seems to be quite over, though."

"I just thought," repeated Mr Haddock, "that I would come down and see if there was anything I could do for you."

"Come in here, Will," said Mrs Haddock, "and take off your collar and lie down."

"Oh, I'm all-right," said Mr Haddock. "I just wanted to see if you—if you——"

But by this time Mrs Haddock had taken him quietly by the arm and sat him down on the edge of his bunk and removed his collar and necktie.

"With a Yo! ho! ho!" sang Mildred softly, as she took off her father's shoes.

"Hush, Mildred," said Mrs Haddock, covering her husband gently with a blanket, and after a while she and Mildred switched off the light and tiptoed out of the room.

Mr Haddock was awakened the next morning by some one knocking on the door.

"Your bath is ready, sir," called a voice. Mr Haddock rubbed his eyes and looked at his watch.

"What bath?" he said, perplexedly trying to think of all the baths he had known, but without success.

"*Your* bath," replied the steward.

"All right," he finally said, and he got out of bed.

Mrs. Haddock and Mildred had gone, leaving what seemed to Mr Haddock a great many women's clothes all over the stateroom.

"This way, sir," said the bath steward.

"Are we on time?" asked Mr Haddock, yawning.

"We lost twenty minutes in the night," said the steward. "The captain fell overboard again."

"Well, well," said Mr Haddock. "He'd better watch out."

"He's very unhappy about it," replied the steward.

"Steward!" yelled a voice.

"Yours is the fifth door down this corridor," said the steward. "Coming, sir!" and he left in the other direction.

"The fifth," said Mr Haddock. "Thank you." And when he had reached the fourth door down the corridor he opened it and went in.

"Oh, I beg your pardon," he said.

"Why, Will Haddock!" exclaimed the lady who was taking a bath. "Think of seeing *you* here."

"Well, if it isn't Nellie Fisher," said Mr Haddock. "Well, well, this *is* a surprise."

"You're just in time, Will," said Nellie. "My soap slipped under the tub."

"With the greatest of pleasure," said Mr Haddock, and he stooped down and felt under the tub until he had recovered the recalcitrant soap, which he handed to Nellie with a magnificent bow and a sweep of his arm.

"Same old Will," said Nellie, giving him a playful pat on the arm.

"You haven't changed much yourself, Nell," said Mr Haddock, glancing into the tub.

"Do you really think so?" asked Nellie. "Henry thinks I'm taking on flesh."

"Nonsense," said Will. "How is Henry, by the way?"

"Oh, just the same," replied Nellie, with a dry laugh. "I left him at home." There was a silence.

"Well," began Mr Haddock, after a few minutes.

"Don't go, Will," said Nellie, "you've just barely come. Here it's been twenty—no, twenty-one years."

"Twenty-one years next March," said Mr Haddock.

"Are you happy, Will?" asked Nellie, trying to reach the middle of her back with a soapy wash rag.

"Oh, sure," said Will. "Here, let me help you."

"Thanks," said Nellie, and then she asked: "Hattie with you?"

"You bet," replied Mr Haddock. "I wouldn't go any place without her. She's the greatest little woman in the world, Nell. And you ought to see little Mildred—she's with us now. Bright as a whip. She'll be eleven next August."

"That's fine, Will," said Nellie, holding out her hand. "I'm awfully glad you're happy."

"Thanks, Nell," said Will, taking her hand. "Well—I guess I'll have to go take my bath now." And then, as he turned to go, he added, "Say, Nellie, I'm sorry about Henry."

"Oh, that's all right, Will," said Nellie. "I'm used to it by now."

"Oh shoot, Will," she added, "I've dropped my soap again."

"I'll get it," said Will, and he did.

"Well, good-by, Will," said Nellie, smiling at him as he handed her the soap.

"Good-by, Nell," said Will, and soon he was in bathroom number 5, quietly soaking in the warm salt water and wondering why the soap didn't seem to lather very well.

"My soap wouldn't lather," he said to Mrs Haddock when he returned and found her and Mildred all dressed. "That's why I took so long."

"Of course it wouldn't," said Mildred, "it was fresh water soap. A child would know that."

"We've had our breakfast already, Will," said Mrs Haddock. "How do you feel this morning? Hungry?"

"Why, I feel all right," said Mr Haddock. "Why shouldn't I? And say, those baths are dandy." And he added, "Oh, by the way, I saw Nellie Fisher this morning."

"Who?" asked Mrs Haddock.

"Nellie Fisher—you remember. My friend back home. She married that man from New York—Henry Kingsbury."

"Oh," said Mrs Haddock, and she stopped brushing her hair. "Oh, yes—Nellie Fisher. Where did you see her, Will?"

Mr and Mrs Haddock Abroad

"In the bath tub," said Mr Haddock. "She was taking a bath."

"Will!" said Mrs Haddock. "You haven't started doing *that* again?"

"No, honest," said Mr Haddock. "I just happened to get into her bathroom by mis take."

"How did she look?" asked Mrs Haddock.

"She's put on a little weight," said Mr Haddock.

"I knew she would," said Mrs Haddock. "Her mother was fat."

"Well! she isn't so terribly that way," said Mr Haddock.

"She's fat," said Mrs Haddock, "and I'll bet that she was clever enough to stay in the bath tub all the time you were there. You're the only person I ever knew who ever thought she was pretty anyway."

Mr Haddock rubbed his chin philosophi-cally.

"I think I'll shave before breakfast," he said. "I hope there is some hot water."

But when Mr Haddock pressed the handle

marked "Hot," and a steady stream emerged, he felt of it and frowned.

"It's cold for June," he announced regretfully.

"Let it run," advised Mrs Haddock, and Mr Haddock let it run.

"Maybe it will warm up towards noon," said Mr Haddock, "when the sun comes out."

"We will be in the Gulf Stream," said little Mildred, "in two or three days."

"I don't think I can wait," said Mr. Haddock, once more running his hand over his chin. "Or can I? Do you think I really need a shave?" he asked Mrs Haddock.

"Yes," said Mrs Haddock.

"Do you, Mildred?" he asked hopefully.

"Yes," was Mildred's candid reply.

"You mustn't say that just because your mother did, Mildred," he said reproachfully. "You must try and think for yourself. You're getting to be quite a big girl now," and with that he pressed a nearby button, and in a minute some one knocked on the door.

"Come in," he called, and the steward entered.

"Steward," said Mr Haddock, "do I need a shave?"

"Step over in this light, please," replied the steward, switching on an electric lamp and taking a small round mirror and headband from his pocket which he adjusted over one eye. "Now—open wide!"

"But I only want to know—" began Mr Haddock.

"Wider," said the steward, and Mr Haddock opened wider, while the steward peered into his throat through a tiny hole in the round mirror.

"Now say 'Ah,' " said the steward.

"Ah," said Mr Haddock.

"But my husband only wanted to know—" began Mrs Haddock.

"Will you step into this other room, please," said the steward, and opening the door he bowed Mrs Haddock and Mildred out.

"Miss Jordan," he called, and a maid came.

"Will you take this lady's history?" said the steward.

"This way, Madam," said Miss Jordan, and the steward closed the door and returned to Mr Haddock.

"Now," said the steward, "again 'Ah.' "

"Ah," said Mr Haddock.

"Ah," said the steward, "I thought so," and he switched off the lamp and pulled the round mirror up onto his forehead. "How long has that been bothering you?"

"About a month," replied Mr Haddock, "although I haven't been sleeping very well for over six weeks."

"Hmmm," said the steward, and he walked over to a small cabinet and began fingering a number of bright instruments, while Mr Haddock watched him apprehensively out of the corner of one eye.

"I hope it isn't anything serious," he said.

"Take off your shirt," replied the steward.

"Yes sir," said Mr Haddock, and he nervously removed his suspenders and shirt.

[115]

Mr and Mrs Haddock Abroad

"The undershirt," said the steward, and Mr Haddock's undershirt came off."

"It was quite warm in May out home," said Mr Haddock, "so I changed to summer underwear earlier than usual. Was that all right?"

The steward did not reply but placed his left ear against Mr Haddock's chest and said "Cough."

Mr Haddock coughed.

"Take off your trousers," said the steward, and Mr Haddock took off his trousers.

"Those veins on the leg are pretty big, aren't they," said Mr Haddock apologetically, "but Doctor Robinson told me——"

"Run around a bit," said the steward brusquely, and Mr Haddock ran around a bit.

"All right," said the steward, "that will do. Now," and he pointed to a card on the opposite wall, "is the bird on that card inside the cage or outside?"

"Outside," replied Mr Haddock, but the

steward looked so surprised that he quickly said "no—inside, inside, doctor."

"Hmmm," said the steward, and he held a piece of colored glass over Mr Haddock's left eye.

"Now," said the steward, "inside or outside?"

"Inside," replied Mr Haddock timidly.

"Sure?" said the steward, rather fiercely.

"Outside—no inside. I'm sure it's inside, doctor," said Mr Haddock.

"Now?" said the steward, and he shifted the glass to the other eye.

"It's rather blurred," said Mr Haddock, "but I think it's inside."

"Hmmm," said the steward, and leaving Mr Haddock standing in the corner he went to the desk and made some notes. Then he blotted the paper briskly, stepped to the door and called, "All right, Miss Jordan," and Miss Jordan ushered in Mrs Haddock and, with some difficulty, Mildred.

"It's about my little girl," said Mrs Haddock. "For some time she has been complaining——"

"Sit down, Madam," said the steward, and with the help of Miss Jordan he grabbed Mildred just as she was bolting for the door and said, "Sit down, little girl—the doctor won't hurt you," and with that he once more switched on his lamp and pulled his round mirror over his left eye and said to Mildred, "Now, little girl—open wide."

"I won't," said Mildred."

"Mildred," said her mother.

"Open wide, little girl," said Miss Jordan, holding her tightly by the shoulder, "and let the nice doctor see if there are any fairies in your throat. Wouldn't you like to see some pretty fairies? Come, little girl—open wide."

"I won't," said Mildred, "and I think it's a dirty trick that, just because father wanted to know whether or not he needed a shave, I've got to have my tonsils out again."

"Will," said Mrs Haddock, "see if you can do anything with Mildred."

"Would it be all right to put my clothes on

now, doctor?" asked Mr Haddock, who had been standing somewhat meekly in one corner, and as the doctor nodded without looking at him, he hastily dressed.

"I don't want anything done with me," said Mildred, squirming in Miss Jordan's grasp. "And you're all big liars, every one of you. You tell me you're going to take me to Europe and the first thing I know I'm in a doctor's office and I bet he takes my tonsils out again and I don't want them out again and I won't have it, I won't! I won't!" and the little girl burst into violent sobs.

"I think she's right," said Mr Haddock, who by now had dressed himself. "And what's more, I would like to complain about there not being any hot water."

"Hot water, sir?" said the steward, "why, yes sir—right here," and he pressed the faucet marked "Cold" and a steaming stream of hot water rushed out.

"Why, it's just like home," said Mr Haddock delighted. "Our upstairs bathroom is just that way."

Mr and Mrs Haddock Abroad

"And here is the morning paper, sir," added the maid, giving him the "Transatlantic Daily News."

"That's like the upstairs bathroom, too, Will," said Mrs Haddock, sarcastically, and turning to the maid, she added, by way of explanation, "I've tried for twenty years to break my husband of some of his bad habits."

"Oh, I guess all men are alike," said the maid jovially. "Well—anything else, sir?"

"No thank you," said Mr Haddock. "Good day," and with that the steward and maid bowed and withdrew.

"Read me the news, Mildred," said Mr Haddock, "while I shave"; and so, as he was lathering his face, Mildred opened the front page of the newspaper, which was published on board ship every day, just like a regular newspaper, and read:

"Pipe Smoking a Favorite Diversion of Many Kings."

"Is that this morning's paper?" asked Mr Haddock. Mildred looked at the date and nodded affirmatively.

Mr and Mrs Haddock Abroad

"Maybe that's only the home edition," suggested Mrs Haddock. "Go on, Mildred."

"New York, June 14." Mildred read: "The growing popularity of pipe smoking in London in recent years recalls the interesting fact that many kings have been enthusiastic followers of this practice, and the collection of pipes of the late Edward VII is said to have been valued at several thousand pounds."

"They must have gotten that by radio," said Mr Haddock. "Try something else."

"Here's a list of famous London fogs," said Mildred, "starting with 1649."

"When was the last one?" asked Mr Haddock, deftly cutting his chin with his safety razor.

"December 5, 1906," said Mildred.

"Just in time for this edition," said Mr Haddock, putting cold water on the cut, and then he added, thoughtfully, "What would our grandfathers and great grandfathers have said if some one had told them that every morning on a ship in the middle of the ocean you could get the very latest news of all that was happening on two continents?"

"It used to take three days," said little Mildred, "to go from New York to Philadelphia, Pennsylvania."

"And now, in three days," said Mr Haddock, "we are—" and he looked out of the stateroom porthole. "Well, it's kind of hard to tell just where we are. The water keeps moving so."

"I don't see how that makes any difference," said Mrs Haddock, and then she added: "Aren't you almost finished, Will?"

"Just finished," he said, and after he had put on his collar and necktie and coat Mrs Haddock and Mildred went out on the deck to walk, and Mr Haddock went in to breakfast.

CHAPTER V

The dining room seemed almost deserted. "Good morning," said Mr Haddock to the waiter, and he obediently sat down in the chair beside which the waiter was standing.

"First of all," said Mr Haddock, "I should like a glass of hot water."

"I find it very effective," said the waiter, tucking the napkin around Mr Haddock's neck.

"Very!" said Mr Haddock.

"Have you ever tried crude oil?" asked the waiter.

"This is to drink," explained Mr Haddock.

"Yes sir!" said the waiter, and then he added, "You shave yourself, sir, don't you?"

"Yes," admitted Mr Haddock

"I thought so," said the waiter. "I can generally tell."

"And after the hot water," said Mr Had-

[123]

dock, "I should like some prunes and some bran flakes——"

"Yes, sir!" said the waiter. "Anything on the face?"

"No!" said Mr Haddock, and so the waiter brought him the stewed prunes.

"And now the bran!" said Mr Haddock.

"Yes sir!" said the waiter, and bending over he said, "Your scalp is very dry, sir."

"Is it?" said Mr Haddock. "That's too bad!"

"A little crude oil—" suggested the waiter.

"Not this time!" said Mr Haddock.

"It wouldn't take long, sir," said the waiter.

"Not this time," repeated Mr Haddock, doggedly.

"Yes sir," said the waiter, and then he added, "Glover's Mange Cure is very good, sir—some prefer it to crude oil."

"No, I think I'll just take bran," said Mr Haddock.

"Very well, sir!" said the waiter, and he brought the toasted bran flakes.

SUDDENLY THE WAITER STOPPED, WHIRLED IN HIS TRACKS AND POINTED HIS
FINGER AT MR HADDOCK. "THEN," HE SHOUTED, "WHERE WERE YOU ON
THE NIGHT OF MARCH FOURTEENTH?"

[125]

Mr and Mrs Haddock Abroad

"And now," said Mr Haddock, "an order of scrambled eggs and a cup of coffee."

"No Glover's?" said the waiter, almost reproachfully.

"No Glover's!" replied Mr Haddock, with a set expression.

"You're sure?" said the waiter, smiling in an ingratiating manner.

"No Glover's!" said Mr Haddock, shaking his head.

"I want to help you," coaxed the waiter.

"No Glover's!" insisted Mr Haddock, stoutly, holding on to the sides of his chair.

The waiter folded his arms and walked up and down in front of Mr Haddock several times.

"No Glover's!" whispered Mr Haddock between tense set lips.

Suddenly the waiter stopped, whirled in his tracks and pointed his finger at Mr Haddock.

"Then," he shouted, "where were you on the night of March fourteenth?"

Mr Haddock gasped and grew pale, but recovered himself.

"No Glover's!" he breathed through clenched teeth.

The waiter bent over the table and shook his finger in his face.

"I'll tell you where you were," he shouted. "I'll tell you where you were! Look at this!" and he suddenly picked up one of the knives from Mr Haddock's table and flashed it in front of his eyes.

"What's this?" he shouted. "What's this?"

"Oh, my God, let me alone! Let me alone!" cried Mr Haddock. "For God's sake, let me alone!"

The waiter straightened up triumphantly, put the knife carefully back in its place, arranged the spoons beside it, and turned to the twelve other waiters.

"Gentlemen," he said—and the dining room suddenly became very quiet, except for the pathetic sobbing of Mrs Glover and her little daughter who, dressed in deep black, had occupied a prominent table all during breakfast.

"Gentlemen," repeated the waiter, "you are

men of intelligence. I wish to appeal to your intelligence, not your emotions. I will not ask you, therefore, to look at that poor woman"— and he pointed to Mrs. Glover—"that poor, heart-broken woman," and his voice fell to a whisper, "that mother!"

"Nor," continued the waiter softly, "will I ask you to look at that little helpless child, for 'Suffer little children'—He said—'to come unto me, and forbid them not' "—and the waiter paused while several of the twelve other waiters wiped their eyes on the napkins which they held over their arms.

"But, gentlemen," said the waiter, and his voice became very hard, "I *will* ask you to look at *that*"—and he pointed to Mr Haddock, cowering white lipped and ashen in his chair—"look at *that,* gentlemen and tell me if any of you—any of you who know what it is to feel a mother's love—any of you who know what it is to have some little grey haired woman waiting and praying and hoping that some day her baby would come back safe and sound—her child whom she had nursed and

[129]

crooned to sleep in its cradle—her boy whom she had perhaps dreamed would one day become President of the United States—gentlemen!" and the waiter paused and went over to Mr Haddock—"Gentlemen, this man once learned the alphabet from his mother's lips and his catechism from his stern old father. I only ask you to look at him," said the waiter, pointing to Mr Haddock, who was by this time sitting very erect. "Look at him," repeated the waiter, and at that moment a ray of sunlight, filtering into the dining room, shone full on Mr Haddock's face, suffusing it with an ethereal glow. "And tell me," continued the waiter, "if that man could do wrong."

Several of the twelve waiters once more began to weep, and Mr Haddock's waiter walked slowly over to them and addressed them.

"Gentlemen," he said, "let me tell you a simple story—the story of a boy who was born in a little log cabin in Ohio some fifty-one years ago—a boy raised on a farm, of poor,

Mr and Mrs Haddock Abroad

God-fearing parents. Of this boy's early struggles I shall say little—of how his mother read the Bible to him every night until he knew every word of the good book by heart—of how he worked on his father's acres by day and studied law by night."

"Gentlemen," went on the waiter, "can you imagine that boy, in his homespun jacket, starting off in the world with nothing in his pocket but the family Bible and a stout heart?"

"But," and he lowered his voice sadly, "need I tell you of the temptations of the world? We are none of us perfect,—and that boy sitting there least of all. But he is like you, gentlemen—he is neither better than you nor worse. And but for that woman there"—and he pointed fiercely at Mrs Glover—"but for that woman there—that vampire—that——"

"Gentlemen," went on the waiter at length, "let each one of you look into your hearts. Let each one of you remember that log cabin, that farm, that homespun jacket and say, 'There, but for the grace of God, go I!' "

"Gentlemen," he concluded, "I thank you!" And he walked over and sat down beside Mr Haddock, while the twelve waiters solemnly filed out of the room.

"I think we've got a chance," he whispered to Mr Haddock, wiping the perspiration off his forehead.

Mr Haddock did not reply, but sat looking straight ahead for many, many minutes.

Finally there was an impressive knock, knock, knock, on the door, and instantly the buzz of whispering died down, and in a deep, ominous silence the door was opened and the twelve returned and took their seats.

Suddenly the leader arose and walked over to where Mr Haddock was sitting.

"William Haddock," he said, "I have the honor of announcing to you that on the twelfth ballot you have been selected by our party to be our candidate for President of the United States."

Instantly the dining room was a scene of

Mr and Mrs Haddock Abroad

tremendous confusion. People leaped on chairs shouting, "Haddock! Haddock!" Flags were waved, hats thrown in the air, and flashlight cameras popped like machine guns. Some Southerners started the rebel yell, and the Dakota delegation replied with Indian war whoops. On the balcony a band struck up "Dixie," and in an instant everyone was on his feet, yelling madly, chanting hysterically, "Haddock! Haddock! Haddock!"

The waiter leaped to his feet and held up his hands for silence.

"Sit down, everybody!" he yelled. "Sit down! Just a minute, please. You're crushing a lot of women against the platform. Stand back—stand back! Sit down, please!"

But the crowd was too hysterically happy to pay any attention. The San Francisco band started playing "Hail, Hail, the Gang's All Here," over in one corner, and the New Jersey delegation, grabbing their standard, fell in behind the musicians and started marching around the hall. From all sides crazy men and women rushed to join the parade and for

[133]

twenty minutes Mr Haddock, flushed and happy, stood on the platform watching the procession march by.

"Get Mrs Haddock and Mildred!" he shouted into the ear of the waiter, "and telegraph the news to my son Frank and my folks, and Mrs. Haddock's folks too."

Finally the band stopped playing and the perspiring people gradually resumed their seats, and then, amid an expectant hush, broken only by the excited clicking of telegraph instruments, Mr Haddock arose.

This was the signal for another frantic outburst of cheering, which lasted for seventeen minutes.

"My friends," said Mr Haddock at last, when quiet had once more been restored, "I am very happy."

Another uproar of cheers broke out, while Mr Haddock smiled and wiped his forehead, and a lady who had come all the way from Butte, Montana, fainted and was carried out.

"My friends," he continued, "I am very happy to accept the great honor and the great responsibility which you have to-day conferred upon me."

"I have only one regret," went on Mr Haddock, "and that is that my father and mother are on our old farm, and not here with me on this platform now."

"God bless 'em!" cried out a lady in a white shirtwaist, and everybody clapped vigorously.

"I did not come here prepared to make a speech," continued Mr Haddock, "and so I will only say at this time that if elected in November I shall pledge myself to a whole-hearted policy in support of those eternal principles which are going to spell certain victory for us when the thinking people of this great nation go to the polls next November."

The rest of Mr Haddock's speech was drowned in a tremendous outburst of cheering, and, waving his hand in farewell, he pushed his way behind the waiter and eight policemen out into the crowd, where he was besieged by a number of reporters and camera men.

"Gentlemen," he cried, laughing, "one at a time, please!"

"Hello there, Bill!" called out a voice.

"Why, it's old Ed!" cried Mr Haddock. "Hey, Ed, you old rascal, come out here and get photographed," and with that Ed Peters, Mr Haddock's boyhood friend, timidly came forward.

"Gosh, it's good to see you!" said Mr Haddock, wringing his hand, and then, turning to the reporters, Mr Haddock said:

"Gentlemen, this is Ed Peters, the best blacksmith in Marietta County, and the man to whose philosophy I owe more than anything else."

And with that there was a great clicking of cameras, and Mr Haddock slapped Ed on the back and asked him if he remembered the first time they smoked a cigar, and told him to be sure to come and see him in the White House, and then, after a few more pictures had been taken of Mr Haddock pitching hay near the Tomb of the Unknown Soldier, he put on his hat and coat and said to the waiter with a happy smile, "Is there a lavatory on this deck?"

And the waiter said, "Yes, sir—right through that door and to the left," and Mr Haddock, choosing his words carefully, said, "Thank you!" and went out amid tremendous cheers, through the door and to the left, and there, kind reader, let us for the present leave him.

CHAPTER VI

The next afternoon about five it began to rain.

"I don't see why it rains at sea," said little Mildred, and, as if to clinch her argument, she said: "Why does it rain at sea?" and, as none of the first-class passengers could tell her, it stopped raining and the sun came out.

But Mr Haddock, who had been sitting alone in the bar for several minutes, suddenly decided what it was he wanted to drink.

"What will you have, Sir?" asked the smoking room steward, shrewdly wiping away all evidence of a former occupant at the table.

"Guess!" said Mr Haddock.

The steward shut his eyes and guessed.

"A martini cocktail?" he said.

Mr Haddock chuckled gleefully.

"No," he said; "guess again!"

Once more the steward shut his eyes.

[138]

Mr and Mrs Haddock Abroad

"A Scotch and soda?"

Mr Haddock clapped his hands and chortled.

"No! No!" he said, grinning triumphantly, and the steward said: "Oh, shoot!"

"You're getting warm, though," said Mr Haddock, encouragingly.

"I perspire a lot," said the steward, "in summer." And then he added: "Is it animal, vegetable or mineral?"

Mr Haddock thought a minute and then said: "Vegetable!"

"Is it something you can touch?" asked the steward.

Mr Haddock bobbed his head up and down in affirmation.

The steward thought a minute and then asked: "Is it in the Northern hemisphere?"

"Yes!" said Mr Haddock.

"Is it in a tunnel?" asked the steward.

"No," replied Mr Haddock.

"Is it in—is it in a trunk?"

"Yes," said Mr Haddock.

"A lady's trunk?" asked the steward.

[139]

"Yes," said Mr Haddock.

"Hum!" said the steward, scratching his head. "Something you can touch—in the Northern hemisphere—in a lady's trunk."

Mr Haddock watched him expectantly, with his eyes glistening with excitement.

"A lemonade!" guessed the steward.

"I said it was vegetable," said Mr Haddock.

"An orangeade?" guessed the steward.

"No," said Mr Haddock. "Wait—I'll act it out."

"All right," said the steward, sitting down while Mr Haddock, chuckling to himself, retired for a minute, only to reappear and announce: "It's two words—this is the first word."

"How many syllables?" asked the steward.

"One," replied Mr Haddock, and he vanished again.

When he once more appeared, after some minutes, he had one of Mrs Haddock's hats on his head, while around his shoulders were two of the curtains from the bed in his stateroom, and in his hand was little Mildred's toothbrush.

"Bronx?" guessed the waiter.

"No!" said Mr Haddock, and he executed a few dance steps, at the same time muttering, "How well you dance, Mrs Gin!"

"Double Bronx?" guessed the waiter.

"No!" said Mr Haddock, and after a minute more of dancing, he said: "The second word is one syllable, too," and ran out of the door in the direction of his stateroom.

When he got there he found, unexpectedly, Mrs Haddock and Mildred.

"William Haddock," said Mrs Haddock, "what are you doing with my hat?"

"I'm playing charades," said Mr Haddock. "And please let me go back."

"Whom are you playing with?" asked Mrs Haddock.

"A fellow," replied Mr Haddock.

"What fellow?" asked Mrs. Haddock.

"Oh, a fellow," replied Mr Haddock. "Please—I said I'd come right back."

"What fellow?" insisted Mrs Haddock.

[141]

Mr and Mrs Haddock Abroad

"Well, he's sort of a steward," replied Mr Haddock.

"Do I know him?" asked Mrs Haddock.

"No," replied Mr Haddock. "I don't think so."

"Where is he steward?" asked Mrs Haddock.

"Well—in the smoking room," said Mr Haddock.

"A bartender!" said Mrs Haddock. "I thought so!"

"No, he isn't," said Mr Haddock. "And please let me go back—he's waiting for me."

"I don't like you to play charades with bartenders," said Mrs Haddock. "And you know it."

"Well, just this once," pleaded Mr Haddock. "I've got a dandy word."

"What?" asked Mrs Haddock, and he leaned over and whispered the word in her ear.

"Well," said Mrs Haddock, "you can go back this once."

"Oh, goody," said Mr Haddock, "and I'll

Mr and Mrs Haddock Abroad

have to borrow Mildred's rain cape for the second syllable."

"You can't have it," said Mildred. "You'll pull it all out of shape."

"No I won't," said Mr Haddock. "Honest!"

"Yes you will," said Mildred, who remembered what had happened to her new brown silk stockings the last time her father had played charades.

"But I've got to use it," said her father.

"What's the word?" asked Mildred, and he whispered the word in Mildred's ear.

"Oh, shoot!" said Mildred. "You could use Mother's umbrella for that."

"Indeed, you'll not!" said Mrs. Haddock.

"Oh, I think you're both just terrible!" said Mr Haddock.

"Well, take my rain cape, then," said Mildred. "Only bring it back right away."

"Oh, sure!" said Mr Haddock, and smiling happily once more, he took the cape and ran back to the smoking room.

"Second word!" he announced through the

door, and putting on the rain cape, he entered.

"This is in the form of a dialogue," he said, and it was.

"Hello there, Pete!" he said in a high, shrill voice, and then taking off the cape, he walked over and took the part of "Pete," who was supposed to be an impecunious old Boston fisherman with a very nervous twitch in his left arm and a wife and four children at home.

"Why, howdy-do, Mrs Arbuthnot," said "Pete." "Sure, and I thought the likes of you was dead!"

"Ha! Ha! Ha!" laughed "Mrs Arbuthnot," shrilly. "Whatever made you think that, Pete?"

"I don't know," replied "Pete."

"That's the first part," announced Mr Haddock. "Now watch closely."

"Well, Mrs Arbuthnot," said "Pete," "whatever are ye wearing that there rain cape for?"

"Why!" replied "Mrs Arbuthnot." "Can't you all guess?"

[144]

"Naw," said "Pete." "I can't guess."

"Because it looks like rain," said "Mrs Arbuthnot."

"Sure, and Oi don't think it will rain," said "Pete," "at all, at all."

"Well, what do you think it will do, for pity's sake?" asked "Mrs Arbuthnot."

"Begorra, and I think it will fizz!" replied "Pete."

"It will what?" interrupted the steward.

"Fizz!" replied Mr Haddock, "but wait; it isn't through yet."

"You say you think it will fizz?" asked "Mrs Arbuthnot," taking off her rain cape.

"Yes, I think it will fizz," replied "Pete."

"That's all!" said Mr Haddock.

"Gin fizz!" said the steward, after a minute.

"Somebody told you," said Mr Haddock, biting his lip.

"No they didn't," claimed the steward, stoutly. "I guessed it."

"All right," said Mr Haddock. "Now you do one."

But before the steward had had time to

[145]

Mr and Mrs Haddock Abroad

think of one, several passengers came into the smoking room, and soon he was quite too busy to play charades with Mr Haddock any more that afternoon.

But after the gin fizz, Mr Haddock really didn't miss the steward so very much, anyway, especially as a very nice, tall gentleman in a naval uniform came in and sat down at the same table with him.

"Do you mind if I sit down here?" he asked.

"Not at all," said Mr Haddock heartily, and then he added: "Haven't I seen you somewhere before?"

"I don't think so," said the gentleman.

"You aren't in the lumber business, are you?" asked Mr Haddock.

"No," replied the other, "I'm not."

"Will you have a drink?" asked Mr Haddock.

"Why, yes—thank you!" replied the stranger, and so Mr Haddock gave the order to the steward for two more gin fizzes.

"My name's Haddock," he said, holding

[146]

out his hand. "I'm in the lumber business—
Haddock & Son."

"My name's Jones," said the other, and they
shook hands cordially.

"How do you think things are going?"
asked the stranger, somewhat timidly, after
a short silence.

"What things?" asked Mr Haddock.

"Well—for instance—this boat?" asked the
other. "Do you think it's going along all
right?"

"Oh, fine!" replied Mr Haddock. "At least
as far as I know. I suppose the captain knows
his business."

"Do you really?" asked the other eagerly.

"Oh, sure!" replied Mr Haddock. "Otherwise he wouldn't be captain."

"That's what I tell them," said the stranger,
and when the steward brought the drinks he
insisted that Mr Haddock take the bigger one.
"You don't know how nice it is to find somebody like you to talk to!" he said.

"Well, it's nice of you to say that," said Mr
Haddock, blushing a little.

"Don't you hate it," went on the stranger, after a few minutes, "when people criticize you a lot?"

"Oh, sure!" said Mr Haddock. "Criticism never helped anybody." And then he added, wisely: "Unless it was helpful criticism."

"You're absolutely right!" said the stranger, "absolutely right! You're a good fellow, Haddock."

"Oh, no, I'm not," said Mr Haddock. "You don't know."

"Yes, I do, Haddock," said the other. "I can tell."

"Say," said Mr Haddock, squirting a little selzer into his glass, "you ought to know Mrs Haddock. There's the greatest little woman in the world, Jones."

"I bet she is," said Jones. "And say, tell me, Haddock—does *she* think everything is going all right with the boat?"

"Oh, sure!" replied Mr Haddock. "And if anything wasn't all right she'd know it, too, right away. Jones, I could tell you more stories about that woman——"

Mr and Mrs Haddock Abroad

"Gee, I'm glad she thinks everything is going all right!" said Jones. "You're not saying that just to be nice?"

"Jones," said Mr Haddock, "I'm not that kind of a fellow. Mrs Haddock will tell you that herself. Why, Jones," said Mr Haddock, "if I started to talk about Mrs Haddock we'd be here all night."

"Gee, I'm pleased," said Jones, and then, leaning over very confidentially, he said: "Haddock, can you keep a secret?"

"Sure," said Mr Haddock.

"No!" said the stranger. "Maybe I better hadn't tell you."

"Oh, go on!" said Mr Haddock.

"No, you'll go tell somebody," said the stranger.

"No, I won't!" insisted Mr Haddock. "Honest! And I'll tell you a secret afterwards, too."

"Well," said the stranger, "if you'll promise not to tell anybody, I'll tell you."

"I promise," said Mr Haddock.

[149]

"Well," said the stranger with a little giggle, "Haddock, I'm the captain."

"No!" exclaimed Mr Haddock.

"Yes, honest!" said the other, bobbing his head up and down. "Look—here's my papers; my name isn't Jones at all—it's Larkin—and here's a picture of me in this uniform, taken on the bridge."

"Well, well," said Mr Haddock, looking at the picture. "I thought I'd seen you before somewhere."

"Where?" asked the captain.

"Well——," said Mr Haddock, hesitating——

"Day before yesterday?" asked the captain, blushing.

"Yes!" said Mr Haddock. "But, shoot! Don't you mind that!"

"I don't mind it," replied the captain, "a bit. Honest, I don't, Haddock. I did it on purpose."

"Of course you did," said Mr Haddock.

"No, you don't believe me," said the captain, looking at Mr Haddock with his big blue eyes.

"Yes, I do!" said Mr Haddock.

"You don't believe I fell overboard on purpose," said the captain, and he looked very unhappy. "Nobody does."

"Yes, I do," said Mr. Haddock, patting him on the back. "And so does Mrs Haddock. Right away when it happened she said, 'Will, I bet he did it on purpose.' "

"Did she, honest?" asked the captain, eagerly.

"Honest Injun," replied Mr Haddock, crossing his heart.

"Gee, that's great," said the captain. "Let's have one more drink."

"No thanks—not for me," said Mr Haddock. "Count me out."

"What else did she say?" asked the captain.

"Oh, she just said she thought you looked too nice a man not to do it on purpose."

"Did she, honest, Haddock?" said the captain, blushing.

"Honest!" replied Mr Haddock. "I wouldn't lie to *you*."

"Haddock," said the captain, "you don't know what it is to have somebody like you I can trust. Honest, Haddock, you don't know what it is to be surrounded by a lot of people who want to criticize you all the time."

"It must be awful!" said Mr Haddock.

"It's perfectly ghastly," said the captain. "I knew the minute I fell overboard that there would be a lot of people who wouldn't understand. But I don't care," said the captain, draining his glass. "I don't care. Friends like that aren't real friends. A thing like this brings out your real friends, Haddock."

"Shake on that, captain," said Mr Haddock, and they shook.

"I suppose there was a lot of talk," said the captain.

"Oh, don't mind that," said Mr Haddock.

"Then there was a lot of talk," demanded the captain instantly.

"No, not a bit!" said Mr Haddock, retreating quickly.

"There better hadn't be," said the captain. "Just wait till they've had a ship to run some day and then they'll understand."

"It must be a lot of work," said Mr Haddock.

"It takes a lot of your time," replied the captain.

"Do you like being captain?" asked Mr Haddock.

"Well, it's all right when you're on land," said the captain.

"Land's a great place," said Mr Haddock. "I was born on land."

"So was I," said the captain.

"Mrs Haddock had an aunt," said Mr Haddock, "who was born with a full head of hair."

"Say, I bet that was wonderful," said the captain.

Just then a sailor came in and saluted.

"Sir, a lady wants to see you right away in the boiler-room," he said to the captain.

"What name?" asked the captain.

"I don't know, Sir," replied the sailor.

"Always get the name," said the captain, and he arose and put on his cap.

"Don't go, Haddock," he said. "I'll be right back. The boiler room isn't far."

"No," said Mr Haddock, "I really think I'd better be getting along. It's almost supper time."

"Well, goodbye, then!" said the captain. "And thanks, awfully. You've helped a lot. And say, I'd like to show you and Mrs Haddock over the ship to-morrow."

"That would be fine, captain," said Mr Haddock, and they shook hands.

"This way, Sir," said the sailor to the captain.

"Oh, I know the way," said the captain, somewhat petulantly, and soon Mr Haddock was left quite alone at his table, so he finished his gin fizz and went down to get ready for dinner.

"Where's my rain cape?" demanded Mildred the instant he put his head inside the stateroom door.

Mr and Mrs Haddock Abroad

"Will," said Mrs. Haddock, "you've been drinking."

"No, I haven't," he said. "Honest! Look!" and he walked along a crack in the carpet and back again just to show Mrs Haddock how steady his feet were.

"Where's my rain cape?" demanded Mildred again.

"I had to loan it to the captain," said Mr Haddock. "He was called to the boiler room quite unexpectedly."

"What captain?" asked Mrs. Haddock.

"The captain of this ship," replied Mr Haddock. "He and I are great friends. He's going to show us over the ship to-morrow."

"Will," said Mrs Haddock, "you've been drinking."

"All right," said Mr Haddock. "Don't believe me. But you'll be sorry some day when I'm dead and a big wreath arrives: 'To old Bill Haddock from his great friend, the Captain.'"

"What is his name?" asked Mrs Haddock.

[155]

Mr and Mrs Haddock Abroad

"Jones," replied Mr Haddock—"or rather, Larkin—yes, Larkin."

"Will Haddock," said Mrs Haddock, "let me smell your breath." So she and Mildred smelled Mr Haddock's breath.

"Gin!" said Mrs Haddock.

"Halitosis!" said Mildred, adding, by way of explanation, "Unpleasant breath."

"Mildred!" said Mrs Haddock, and then she added: "Hurry up, Will—Mildred and I will go on ahead."

When they had gone Mr Haddock began to wash, and while he was drying his face his eye was caught by a full-page advertisement in the magazine which Mildred had been reading when he came into the room.

"He Just Didn't Have Sex Appeal," said the ad., and above that proclamation was the picture of a disconsolate middle-aged gentleman in a dress suit who was gazing mournfully at a telegram.

Mr Haddock read on, with rising curiosity.

"Bill Jones," explained the ad., "was a good fellow, a success in business and popular with the boys at the office. But somehow he never seemed to be able to make good socially. He often wondered what it was about him that made women seem to avoid him. And then one day a friend, more frank than the others, sent him a telegram and told him why.

" 'You Just Haven't Got Sex Appeal,' " was the message.

Mr Haddock got up, looked in the mirror, and said "Gosh!" Then he read the page through once more.

"You Never Can Be Sure," concluded the ad., in large black accusing letters. "You Never Can Be Sure."

"Gosh!" said Mr Haddock again, and he sank onto the bunk. Finally he reached a decision. Trembling a little, he pressed a button.

"Send me a maid," said Mr Haddock when the steward opened the door.

"Yes Sir," replied the steward.

While he was waiting for the maid Mr Haddock looked once more in the mirror and carefully adjusted his necktie. He was interrupted by a knock.

"Come in," said Mr Haddock, and the door opened.

"Ah, how do you do," said Mr Haddock, smiling cordially, but his heart sank when the maid stayed in the door-way and said, "What is it you want?"

"Won't you come in?" he asked invitingly.

"What is it you want?" repeated the maid, not moving.

"I want," said Mr Haddock, thinking very quickly, "to show you my collection of old coins."

"Oh, let me see them," said the maid and she entered, while Mr Haddock, holding his breath, nervously opened his trunk and took out all his old coins.

"Oh—here's a Portuguese 1580!" exclaimed the maid in glee. "And here's a 1740 Greek drachma!"

"Very rare," said Mr Haddock, at the same time clenching his fists and beginning to breathe very deeply and passionately.

"What are you doing?" asked the maid, looking up.

"Nothing," mumbled Mr Haddock. "I just thought I saw a moth."

"Where did you get this—this piastre?" cried the girl. "Why—it's a real Turkish piastre!"

"Very rare," said Mr Haddock and then, while the girl was engaged in deciphering the date of the coin, he quickly narrowed his eyes and leered at her.

"Well," said she, getting up almost instantly, "I'm afraid I'll have to be going."

Mr Haddock grew pale.

"Oh—must you?" he stammered.

"Yes," she replied, and Mr Haddock backed away from her nervously.

"Goodbye!" he said, "and thanks for coming."

"I would stay longer——," she began.

"Oh, no, don't, really," he said quickly. "I know just how you feel," and her look of gratitude made him wince.

"You must come down and see my coins some time," said the maid at the door.

"I would like to," said Mr Haddock, "but perhaps——"

"I've got something very rare to show you, too," said the maid, smiling invitingly. "Please come!"

But when she had gone he sank down on his bunk and put his face in his hands.

Could he be sure?

He groaned.

If he could only be sure.

Suddenly he got up resolutely and pressed the button.

"Yes, Sir?" said the steward.

"Send me another maid," he said.

"Yes, Sir!" replied the steward, but in a few minutes he returned empty handed.

"The maids are all at dinner," he announced. "Would the sempstress do?"

"All right," said Mr Haddock. "Send me the sempstress."

With head bowed in hands, Mr Haddock waited. Finally there came a knock, and his

heart leaped violently and began to pound.
"Come in!" he said, and the door opened.

The sempstress was quite a bit larger than
the maid. In fact she was one of the largest
women Mr Haddock had seen for eight
months.

"Won't you come in?" he asked.

"What for?" she demanded.

Mr Haddock cleared his throat and said:
"I want to show you something nice."

"Yes you do!" said the sempstress, sneering
and folding her arms.

"Honest!" said Mr Haddock, and leaning
forward confidentially he whispered: "I've
got a Turkish piastre."

The sempstress laughed somewhat coarsely
at that.

"You've got a what?" she demanded.

"All right!" said Mr Haddock, with dignity. "If you don't want to come in, you
don't have to."

"You bet I don't!" said the sempstress.

"Well, I didn't say you did," said Mr Haddock.

"You bet you didn't!" said the sempstress.

"Well, I could make you come in if I wanted to," said Mr Haddock.

"Yes, you could!" said the sempstress.

"I could!" said Mr Haddock.

"Couldn't!" said the sempstress.

But before he said "I could" again, Mr Haddock suddenly remembered that one of the first rules of salesmanship is that the customer is always right.

"You're right!" he said.

"You bet I'm right!" she replied, somewhat adversely.

"Well, I said you were right," said Mr Haddock, a little irritated.

"You bet you said I was right!" said the sempstress.

Mr Haddock recovered himself and smiled suddenly.

"And how are those youngsters?" he asked.

"What youngsters?" asked the sempstress, suspiciously.

"Your little children," replied Mr Had-

[162]

dock. "Don't tell me you didn't bring them with you."

"I ain't got any children," said the sempstress.

"Are you sure?" said Mr Haddock, and then he laughed. "Of course," he said, "how stupid of me! But I always get you confused with Mrs Henderson."

"Mrs who?" asked the sempstress.

"Mrs Henderson," replied the wily Mr Haddock. "A charming woman. A great deal like you. But she hasn't your figure."

"What's the matter with my figure?" asked the sempstress.

"Nothing," replied Mr Haddock, wiping perspiration from his forehead. "It's wonderful!"

"It'll do," said the sempstress.

"Of course it will do," said Mr Haddock, "and don't you let anybody tell you it won't. Why, only the other day I heard somebody say she wished she had your figure."

"Who?" demanded the sempstress.

"Well, it doesn't matter who," said Mr

Haddock. "But it was somebody pretty high up. And she said you had a very religious nature and were fond of grapefruit," and he held out a basket of fruit temptingly arranged.

"I don't like grapefruit," said the sempstress.

"Or was it oranges?" said Mr Haddock. "I always get them confused."

"Well, I'll take an orange," said the sempstress.

"Take a lot," said Mr Haddock. "Take a dozen. There's plenty more where those come from."

"Well," said the sempstress, hesitating, "I don't know——"

"That's just where I come in," said Mr Haddock. "I do know. I'm paid to know. Let me show you the certified figures for the period ending May, 1924," and he pulled out a little note book.

"Let me see!" said Mr Haddock. "You would come under Group B—yes—Group B —that was what we called Group A last year.

Mr and Mrs Haddock Abroad

Now with us," said Mr Haddock, becoming more and more convincing, "you could take at your age—let me see—34, isn't it?"

"Forty-four," said the sempstress, "next August."

"No, really!" said Mr Haddock, with an ingratiating smile. "Well, well, you certainly don't look it. I certainly wouldn't put you a day over thirty-four. Well, well!" And then he added: "My little girl's birthday's in August, too."

"Now," he said, turning over the pages of his note book, "here we are—Group B, with modified death clause—at your age you could easily take a dozen oranges now—and next year, of course, you could take another dozen. But I would really recommend," said Mr Haddock, seriously, "that you take advantage of that extra half dozen now, which is, as you know, accumulative——"

"Do I have to sign anything?" asked the sempstress.

"Ah, bless your heart," said Mr Haddock, "that's what they all want to know. It re-

minds me of the story about the two English-
men——"

"What do I have to sign?" asked the sempstress.

"Nothing!" replied Mr Haddock. "Absolutely nothing, my dear lady. All you have
to do is to step inside here and take your
oranges. Doesn't that sound fair? Could
anything be fairer? Just say so, madam, and
I'll throw the oranges out the window," and
he made a pass as though to hurl the basket
through the porthole.

"Don't do that," cried the sempstress, grabbing the basket.

"All right, madam," said Mr Haddock,
"you'll take the oranges. Good! And I'm
sure you'll never regret it. Now just sit down
in this chair, please," and Mr Haddock politely conducted the sempstress to the chair
and, when he had seated her, removed her hat
and put it carefully on the bed.

"Now," he said, "just relax, please——,"
and then he looked up and saw Mrs Haddock
standing in the doorway watching him.

Mr and Mrs Haddock Abroad

"Good evening, dear!" he said, putting the sempstress' hat back on her head. "I'm so glad you came just at this minute."

"William!" said Mrs Haddock.

"This lady," explained Mr Haddock, "has met with an accident, an unfortunate accident."

Mrs Haddock did not respond.

"It seems that two years ago," continued Mr Haddock, "she was crossing a street where there was a great deal of traffic, and in the general confusion she was thrown off her bicycle onto the ground and rendered unconscious, and from that day until this she has not been able to recover her memory."

Mrs Haddock remained standing in the doorway.

"For years," went on Mr Haddock, "she wandered over the face of the globe, searching far and wide for her fiancé who had been on the bicycle with her at the time of the accident. At times she believed him dead; at times, alive. Imagine it!"

[167]

Mrs Haddock showed no signs of imagining it.

"Finally," said Mr Haddock, "she heard in Melbourne, Australia, that he was on this boat——"

"William," said Mrs Haddock, "we are waiting for you at dinner."

"Yes, dear," said Mr Haddock, and so, bowing and asking the sempstress to please excuse him while he went into dinner, Mr Haddock put on his shirt and coat and, with a cheery "All ready, dear!" he fell in behind Mrs Haddock and followed her to the dining room, whistling loudly and happily as he went.

CHAPTER VII

"This," said the captain, opening a door, "is the second class smoking room, and *that,*" said he, pointing to a man seated at the table, "is a second class passenger."

"Oh, really," said Mrs Gerrish. "A second class passenger. Well, well," and she went up to the man and examined him carefully with a lorgnette which always hung from a conspicuous spot on her neck.

The captain, true to his promise of the preceding afternoon, was engaged in showing Mr and Mrs Haddock and little Mildred over the ship. With them, by one of those curious coincidences which happen only at sea, was Mrs Gerrish—Mrs John ("Slugger") Gerrish—who was from Boston and very proud of her ancestry.

"And so you're a second class passenger?" she said.

"Yes, ma'am," said the man, rising to his feet and putting down his copy of the Atlantic Monthly.

"Well, well," said Mrs Gerrish. "And are you happy here? Do you get good food?"

"Yes, ma'am," replied the man, with a shifty glance at the captain. "They treats us all right."

"And how did you happen to get here?" asked Mrs Gerrish in a kindly voice.

"Well, ma'am," said the man, "it's a long story. It was drink done it."

"How unfortunate," breathed Mrs Gerrish.

"Yes, ma'am," said the second class passenger. "Drink."

"Well, well," said Mrs Gerrish. "Do go on," and turning to the other passengers, she said: "Isn't this interesting?"

"Well, ma'am," said the man, "I was working in a factory and one day I was called home and my wife had a baby."

"Indeed," said Mrs Gerrish, drawing away her skirts just a little.

"Yes, ma'am," said the man. "And so I got

a job in another factory and then, about nine months later, I was called home and my wife had another baby."

"Indeed," said Mrs Gerrish.

"Yes, ma'am," said the man. "And so we left that town and went somewhere where we could forget. But we hadn't been in the new town more than a year when one day I was called home and found——"

"That your wife had had another baby?" suggested little Mildred.

"Yes, ma'am," said the man, "and so I began to drink."

"My poor man," said Mrs Gerrish, putting her hand on his shoulder. "Don't lose hope."

"Hope?" said the man, bitterly. "Not for the likes of me, ma'am. I'll always be a second class passenger. You don't know how it is, once you get started. But my children—I want my children to have a chance."

"Is your wife on board?" asked Mr Haddock.

"Yes, sir," said the man.

"I'd sort of like to see her," said Mr Haddock, with much interest.

"Will!" said Mrs Haddock.

The second class passenger blushed and lowered his eyes.

"She can't see anybody now," he said, "because——"

Mr Haddock shook his head.

"I understand," he said.

"Thank you, sir," said the man, and turning to Mrs Gerrish he said: "Is that all, ma'am?"

"Quite," said Mrs Gerrish, moving away. "Almost too much, I might say," and the others followed her.

"Now then," said the captain briskly, leading them through a door into a large passage way, "shall we go down into the bowels of the ship?"

"Captain, please," said Mrs Gerrish, wincing audibly, and giving him a look which would have spelled disaster had he been trying to do anything in a social way in Boston that year.

The captain was instantly covered with confusion, but he bravely stuck to his guns and decided to see it through.

"Madam," he said in the embarrassed silence which followed Mrs Gerrish's remark, "I'm just a simple sea captain like my grandfather before me. I was born August 4, 1875, in a small town near South Bend, Indiana. My early education was received in the South Bend public schools, except for one year when I was sick and studied at home. At the age of eighteen I entered Holy Cross College, where I devoted myself to literary work and track athletics. Upon graduation I went into the bond business for one year and then decided to take up the sea as a career. My favorite author is Kipling; my favorite actress, Maude Adams. I think that Sidney Carton, in the 'Tale of Two Cities,' is the greatest character in fiction, and that Edison is perhaps our greatest living American.

"Now, then," continued the captain, doggedly, "shall we go down into the bowels of the ship?"

You could have heard a pin drop, and just

[173]

at that moment Mrs Haddock dropped a pin and all jumped nervously.

"I heard a pin drop," said Mr Haddock, in an attempt to relieve the tension.

"I don't care if you heard a hundred pins drop," said the captain, who by this time was quite pale, and trembling with nervous excitement.

"Well, I didn't mean it as a criticism," said Mr Haddock.

"Now, Will," whispered Mrs Haddock, "don't you get into this."

But just at that moment the faint blast of a whistle was heard way up above them and suddenly, at both ends of the passage way, great iron doors dropped down with an ominous clang.

"Great heavens!" said the captain, looking at his wrist watch, "I forgot," and he rushed to one of the iron doors and began pounding on it and shouting, "Hey, Oscar!—Oh, Oscar! —say, Oscar, listen—this is the captain—hey, O S C A R!"

But no Oscar answered.

[174]

"Try 'Frank,' " suggested Mr Haddock, "or 'Bobbie.' "

The captain shook his head and ran to the other door.

"Hey, OSCAR!" he yelled.

"Oh, dear," said Mrs Haddock.

"Let me out of here, captain," said Mrs Gerrish, "or I shall report you."

"I can't let you out, madam," said the captain.

"What's the matter?" asked Mr Haddock.

"It's a collision drill," said the captain, "and we're caught in a water-tight compartment."

"Oh, that's all right," said Mr Haddock, jovially. "I don't mind water-tight compartments a bit. And my daughter, you know, is a Girl Scout."

"Yes, I know," said the captain, "but it's only the captain who can give the signal for the drill to be over and if I'm not there to give the signal——"

"You mean——," said Mrs Haddock.

[175]

"Precisely," said the captain. "We may be in here for weeks."

"Oh, dear," said Mrs Haddock. "And I left the window of my stateroom open."

The Haddocks looked at each other in dismay.

"We may have to eat one of us," whispered the captain, "before it is over," and he and the Haddocks glanced at Mrs Gerrish, who was pacing nervously up and down in front of the farther door.

"Captain," said Mrs Gerrish, stopping suddenly, "we must organize."

"Yes, ma'am," said the captain. "I'll be captain."

"All right," said Mrs Gerrish. "Now I suggest that you appoint a temporary committee of one——"

"I appoint you," said the captain.

"Well," said Mrs Gerrish, blushing modestly. "If you all agree——"

"We agree," said Mr Haddock and the captain.

Mr and Mrs Haddock Abroad

"Why, we don't either," said Mrs Haddock, starting forward.

"Thank you," said Mrs Gerrish. "I accept, and I shall try to do my best. Now—do you all agree that our meetings shall be governed by Robert's rules of order?"

"Yes," said the captain and Mr Haddock.

"No," said Mrs Haddock.

"Why not?" asked Mr Haddock.

"You know well enough why not," said Mrs Haddock. "And, Will Haddock, I'll bother you to keep your nose out of this."

"Well, why not Robert's rules of order?" asked the captain. "What other rules of order do you want?"

"I don't know," said Mrs Haddock. "What other rules of order are there?"

"I think," said Mrs Gerrish, in businesslike tones, "that we shall save a lot of time today by temporarily adopting Robert's rules of order and then later perhaps we can refer this request of our second vice-president, Mrs Haddock, to the proper committee."

Mr and Mrs Haddock Abroad

"Gee, Hattie," said Mr Haddock, "you're second vice-president. That's great."

"Who's first vice-president?" asked Mrs Haddock.

"The position of first vice-president," said Mrs Gerrish, "is temporarily vacant," and with that she drew out from her bosom a copy of Robert's rules of order and beat on the table with her gavel.

"The meeting will come to order," she said, and the meeting came to order, all except Mildred.

"Sit down and keep quiet, little girl," said Mrs Gerrish, "or I shall have to ask the sergeant-at-arms to put you out."

"Out where?" asked Mildred, and the president, by way of reply, beat very loudly on the table and cried, "Order!"

"Now," she said, "the first thing will be the reading of the minutes of the last meeting. Our brother-secretary, Mr Haddock, will please oblige with the minutes of the last meeting."

"But," said Mr Haddock, somewhat bewildered, "there wasn't any last meeting."

"There must have been a last meeting," said Mrs. Gerrish, severely, "or we couldn't have gotten as far as we have with our present campaign."

"What campaign?" asked Mildred.

"Order," cried the lady president, and then she leaned over the table and said, "I must remind you all that our time is somewhat limited and I would therefore request that you oblige me and my colleagues by refraining from unnecessary questions until the debate is thrown open to the house. Am I understood?"

"Yes," said Mr Haddock and the captain.

"Very well then," said Mrs Gerrish, and turning to Mr Haddock she said, "Now—please—the minutes of the last meeting."

So Mr Haddock read the minutes of the last meeting.

"The regular monthly meeting," he read, "of the St. Nicholas Fire, Plate Glass and Outing Society——"

"Don't try to be funny," said the lady president, so Mr Haddock started again.

"The regular monthly meeting," he read, "of the Westchester County Fire, Plate Glass and Outing Society was held in the clubrooms on Friday, May 24. Present—lady President Mrs Gerrish, lady Second Vice-President Mrs Haddock and daughter, Brother Secretary William Haddock, and the Captain. Absent —Resident members Wiley, Auchincloss, Beedy, Reynolds, F. Messersmith, P. Messersmith, Jordan, Tompkins, Lovett, Gurney, Pratt, and all the non-resident members except Shea, Donahue, Forbes, Lawrence, Twedle——"

"Tweedle," said the lady president, correcting his pronunciation.

"It's spelled with one 'e' " said Mr Haddock.

"Tweedle," said the lady president.

"Tweedle," continued Mr Haddock, "Mumford and Gloucester."

"Which Gloucester?" asked the lady president.

"Gloucester P. A.," replied the secretary.

"All right," said the lady president. "Go on."

"The meeting was opened with the marching song," began Mr Haddock.

"That's right," said the lady president. "I forgot our marching song. Stand up, everybody," so they all stood up and sang the song of which I shall only reproduce the verses and the chorus.

Marching Song:—Let Us Not Be Too Much Up and Down.

Air:—Verse—Hot Time in the Old Town To-night.

Chorus—Annie Laurie.

1st Verse.

When everything is going bad and you are out
    at sea
And love's sweet dream lies shattered at your
    feet
And the shells are whizzing past you, and you
    haven't a cent to your name
And everyone you meet seems someone else
And you are blue on account of all that.

Mr and Mrs Haddock Abroad

Chorus.
Don't be blue
Don't be blue.
Don't be blue on account of all that.

Steady hearts and loyal eyes are watching over
    all
So don't be blue on account of all that.

2nd Verse.
A member and his friend were standing on a
    street corner one day
Waiting for a street car which was coming
    along very fast
While out at sea a storm was raging with all
    its might and main
And down at Washington they were making
    laws for you and me
But to him she softly said.

Chorus.
Don't be blue, etc.

"Now, again," said Mrs Gerrish, when they

had finished. "And everybody get into it this time—I mean you, Mrs Haddock."

And so they sang the song once more until the veritable welkin of the bulkhead rang.

"That's fine," said Mrs Gerrish, flushed with success.

"Now continue with the minutes, please," and Mr Haddock continued.

"After the song," read Mr Haddock, "came the reading of the minutes of the last meeting —do I have to read those, too?" he asked, looking up at Mrs Gerrish.

"Not this time," said the lady president. "Go on."

"This was followed," continued Mr Haddock, "by the report of the Finance Committee which was accepted. Following this came the report of the Committee on New Members which was accepted. Mr Ellison then read the report of the Committee on Old Members which was accepted after much heated discussion and the ejection from the hall of brother members McCurdy, Grotch, O'Hara (3), Ferguson, Pomeroy, Hart, El-

[183]

kins and Dooley. The debate was then thrown open to the house and the meeting adjourned without the customary refreshments and prayer. Respectfully submitted, William Haddock—Secretary Pro Tem."

"I move the minutes be accepted as read," said the captain, rising to his feet, and the minutes were accepted as read.

"That brings us to 'Unfinished Business,'" said the lady president, "and first under the head of 'Unfinished Business' I should like to read a poem which I have written since our last meeting."

The captain jumped to his feet.

"I move," he said, "that the poem be accepted as read."

"I second that," shouted Mr Haddock.

"But I haven't read it yet," objected Mrs Gerrish.

"I move a vote of thanks to Mrs Gerrish," said Mr Haddock.

"I move it be made unanimous," said the captain, and so amid much applause the poem was accepted as read and a unanimous vote of

[184]

thanks was incorporated in the minutes and the secretary was instructed to draw up a copy and send it to Mrs Gerrish and all the members of her immediate family.

"Next unfinished business," demanded Mr Haddock quickly, when the applause had died down.

"The next unfinished business," said Mrs Gerrish, "is the debate."

"What debate?" asked Mr Haddock.

"Resolved," said Mrs Gerrish, reading off a slip of paper, "that more harm than good is done by——"

"By what?" asked the captain.

"It doesn't say," replied Mrs Gerrish, turning over the slip.

"It doesn't matter," said Mr Haddock, "I'll take the negative."

"That only leaves the affirmative for me," complained the captain, but Mr Haddock had already started.

"Ladies and gentlemen," he said, "there is one point in connection with the subject before us to-night which my worthy opponent seems to have quite overlooked.

"My friends," went on Mr Haddock, pointing his finger at the captain. "I just want to ask my worthy opponent one thing. I just want to ask him one thing and then I will rest my case. One thing," and Mr Haddock began searching through the pile of books which were beside him on the table. "One thing," he repeated, and he held book after book upside down and shook them and wiped perspiration from his forehead and looked under the tables and started frantically through the books again.

"I just want to ask him one little——" he began.

"Time's up," said Mrs Gerrish, hitting the table with her gavel. "Captain Larkin will have five minutes for the affirmative," and as Mr Haddock sank into his chair the captain arose and bowed with a confident smile.

"I think I can answer my worthy opponent's question," he said, "and I think that the answer is 'yes'. I, too, have made a careful study of the immigration figures both during President Cleveland's administration and after, and if my opponent can look me in the eye and say that with all our so-called modern improvements—our telephones, our radios, our automobiles, our express trains—we are any better or happier than they were in the time of Plato and Aristotle—if my worthy opponent can say that, then my worthy opponent is just a cockeyed liar," and with that the captain walked over and shook hands with Mr Haddock and they both smiled happily and sat down while the vote was being counted.

"As a result of the vote," announced the lady president, "the vote resulted as follows: Haddock 2, Larkin 0. The decision, therefore, rests with the affirmative."

"But I had the negative," protested Mr Haddock.

"No you didn't," said Mrs Gerrish "you had the negative last week. My heartiest congratulations," and she leaned over and shook his hand warmly while he arose and bowed in response to the scattered applause.

"And now, O Lord," said Mrs Gerrish, closing her eyes and gazing upwards, "and now, O Lord——"

"Aren't there any refreshments?" demanded little Mildred loudly.

"Shhh," said Mr Haddock, bowing his head.

"But——" said little Mildred.

"Shhh," said Mrs Gerrish, with closed eyes, and all the subscribers for the Friday afternoon series turned around and glared at the little girl.

"Oh, don't you shshsh *me*," said little Mildred. "I'm hungry."

Mrs Gerrish waited.

"And now, O Lord——" she began.

"Then there aren't any refreshments?" said Mildred.

Mrs Gerrish waited again.

"Well, what a lousy meeting *this* is," said Mildred, and after that she lapsed into a gloomy silence while Mrs Gerrish prayed.

"Amen," said Mr Haddock, conservatively, at the conclusion of the prayer.

"Have I forgotten anything?" whispered Mrs Gerrish to the captain. The captain considered thoughtfully a minute.

"God bless papa and mama," he said.

"God bless papa and mama," repeated Mrs Gerrish.

"And make me——" said the captain.

"And make me a good girl," said Mrs Gerrish. "Amen."

"Amen," said Mr Haddock and the captain.

"I move," said the captain, "that the prayer be accepted as read."

"Accepted by whom?" asked little Mildred.

"I second the captain's motion," said Mr Haddock, and so the prayer was accepted as read.

"The debate is now thrown open to the house," said Mrs Gerrish, and there was a silence.

"I suggest," said the captain, "that we take a vote."

"What on?" asked Mrs Haddock.

"Anybody second that?" said Mrs Gerrish, and as nobody responded she said, "It has been moved and seconded that we take a vote. All in favor say 'Aye'—contrary-minded—the 'Ayes' have it," and she began tearing up slips of paper and passing them around.

"But what are we voting on?" asked Mr Haddock, bewildered.

"Have you got a pen?" asked Mrs Gerrish.

"No," said Mr Haddock.

"A pencil will do," she replied, "and please write clearly," and she passed on.

Mr Haddock turned to the captain, who was scribbling away very busily.

"Whom or what should I vote for?" he asked.

"Vote for one," said the captain, and went on writing.

"One what?" asked Mr Haddock, and as the captain paid no attention he went up to the desk.

"Please, Mrs. President," he said, "whom should I vote for?"

"Vote for one," she replied. "It's the Australian ballot."

"Oh," said Mr Haddock, relieved, and he had just time to put a cross on his paper when Mrs Gerrish called, "Time's up," and snatched the ballot out of his hand. "Time's up," she said again, and passing rapidly around the room she collected all the ballots and put them in a box on the desk.

"Now," she said, "I think that clears up the unfinished business. Next we will take up new business. Has any one any new business to bring up at this time?"

Nobody responded.

"Well, then," said Mrs Gerrish, "I should like with your permission to bring up a matter which is of interest to all of us and which has not been discussed, I believe, before this afternoon. It is a matter which is, in my opinion, sufficiently important at this time to warrant our taking at least a few minutes for informal discussion before the meeting adjourns. "I refer," said Mrs Gerrish, "to the question of how we are going to get out of this watertight bulkhead."

This remark was greeted with interest.

"Now the first thing in every case like this," said Mrs Gerrish, "is intelligent organization and so I hereby appoint a committee consisting of Mr Haddock and the captain to investigate this condition, and I should like now to have the report of that committee."

Mr Haddock slowly arose.

"Mrs President," he said, and she bowed and sat down. "Mrs President and members," continued he, "we have unfortunately not had quite as much time for the preparation of this report as we had hoped. Mrs Haddock has not been well all spring and my colleague has unfortunately been called out of town rather more often than usual in connection with unexpected duties involved in the running of this ship. Nevertheless," said Mr Haddock, taking out a pair of horn-rimmed glasses and adjusting them to his nose, "I will read you what we have accomplished so far," and he took from his pocket a neatly typewritten manuscript of some fifty-two odd pages.

"I shall omit the preamble," he said, turning over the first twenty-eight pages, "and get right down to the meat of the matter."

"Good," said little Mildred, and Mr Haddock began to read.

"This situation in 1912," he read, "therefore presented the following peculiar counter-situation. Out of four hundred and fifty-two stations on the Pacific coast, three hundred and twenty-nine were operated entirely by gas, and of the remainder only sixty-eight were what is termed 'all electric,' by which is meant that only from 55 to 70 per cent of their power was obtained by the use of gas or its by-products. Of the personnel of these stations," went on Mr Haddock, "the percentage in 1912 was largely white, as shown by the following figures: Whites, 436,394; Negroes, 1; Chinese, 0; Japanese, 0; Indians, 0.

"I might add," said Mr Haddock, looking up and taking off his nose-glasses for an instant, "that the negro later died."

[193]

Mr and Mrs Haddock Abroad

"Well, well," said Mrs Gerrish, sympathetically.

"That," said Mr Haddock, "brings us down to 1924, and in that connection I must tell you an interesting story of what happened to Mrs Haddock and myself shortly before the completion of this report. We had been playing tennis all morning in the hot sun and at lunch Mrs Haddock somewhat foolishly ate a can of corned beef hash, and two dishes of ice cream with some new kind of maple walnut sauce. After lunch we picked up our canoe and started walking overland in order to reach Big Walnut by night, where we could get gasoline and fresh provisions, as we were running rather low at the time. But as Mrs Haddock began to complain soon of feeling tired, we put up for the night at a farm house on the way and here is the interesting part of this story," said Mr Haddock, once more removing his glasses and smiling. "That farmer," he said impressively, "was an old Pennsylvania Railroad man and had been with the company for twenty-seven years and knew

[194]

every inch of the line between Buffalo and Schenectady as well as you or I know our first names."

"Well, well," said Mrs Gerrish.

"But to continue," said Mr Haddock, "and I hope you younger people will pardon me for having related that little anecdote which was to me very interesting at the time and I think, for some of you at least, very significant."

"Now," he said, turning to the last page of his report, "to summarize; three plans for getting out of this watertight bulkhead have therefore been submitted to date.

"The first of these, submitted anonymously, involves dropping little Mildred out of a porthole, in the hopes that perhaps the splash or her outcries would attract attention. This was rejected by the committee on the ground that there is unfortunately no porthole in this part of the ship."

"The second plan was much more ingenious, I thought," volunteered the captain.

"Who submitted it?" asked Mrs Gerrish, interestedly.

The captain blushed. "Well, I sort of thought of it," he admitted.

"What is the third plan?" asked little Mildred.

"Don't you want to hear my plan?" asked the captain, crestfallen.

"Not if it's like the first one," said little Mildred. "I certainly didn't think much of that."

"Go on, Captain," said Mrs Haddock. "Don't mind her. Tell them your plan."

"Well," said the captain, "my plan rather ingeniously makes use of radio. Have you got a piece of chalk, Mrs Gerrish?"

"I think so," said Mrs Gerrish, feeling in her pockets.

"Here's one," said Mrs Haddock. "Is yellow all right?"

"Yellow will do, I think," said the captain, and taking the chalk he drew a rather complicated diagram on the side of the wall, somewhat as follows:

[196]

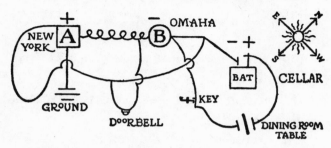

"Now," he said, "do you know anything about radio?"

"My son got Pittsburgh one night," said Mr Haddock, "but there was a lot of static."

"What were they playing?" asked Mrs Gerrish.

"It was some sort of a jazz band," said Mr Haddock.

"I like opera best," said Mrs Gerrish, and she hummed a few of the more important notes from "Faust." "That's from 'Rigoletto.' "

"There's a wonderful old fiddler out home," said Mrs Haddock. "He could make a thousand dollars if he went into some musical show down in New York—it said so in the paper one morning."

Mr and Mrs Haddock Abroad

"I like banjo music best," said Mr Haddock.

"Did you ever hear Caruso?" asked Mrs Gerrish.

"If you don't mind——" said the captain, coughing timidly.

"Oh, excuse us——" they cried.

"Now, then," said the captain, pointing to his diagram.

"I don't think that will work, Captain," said Mrs Gerrish.

"Why not?" asked the captain.

"Well, go on—I'll tell you later," she replied.

"Tell me now," he urged.

"No," she replied. "I just don't think it will work."

The captain bit his lip and looked very sad.

"Go ahead, Captain," said Mr Haddock, "don't you mind."

"No, she don't think it will work," said the captain.

"Oh, sure, she thinks it will work," said Mr Haddock.

"No she doesn't," said the captain. "You go on tell them your plan," and he went over and sat down in a chair and began to bite his fingernails.

"Well," said Mr Haddock, "my plan was not as scientific as the captain's, but I'm just a business man—I'm in the lumber business," he said with a smile, to Mrs Gerrish. "Here's my business card."

"Oh, yes," said Mrs Gerrish. "I've always wanted to meet somebody in the lumber business," and she took the card and dropped it into the waste basket.

"Now, then, as I say," went on Mr Haddock, "I'm just a plain business man——"

"Oh, get on with it, Will," said Mrs Haddock. "We're all starved."

"My plan in brief," said Mr Haddock, giving his wife a resentful look, "is to send a message to somebody else on this ship."

"Oh, that's a wonderful plan," said Mrs Gerrish. "What will we say in the message? Wait—I'll get a piece of paper and a pencil."

"I thought of that plan too," said the captain, but nobody paid any attention to him, so he continued biting his nails moodily.

"Now," said Mrs Gerrish, "what will we say?"

"Must it be in ten words?" asked Mrs Haddock.

"We might send a night letter," suggested Mrs Gerrish.

"No—let's get it to them right away," said Mrs Haddock, "it won't cost so much more."

"Well, then—ten words," said Mrs Gerrish, and she started to write.

"My plan was something like that," said the captain. "It consisted in——"

"Here—how's this?" said Mrs Gerrish triumphantly, and she read, "Am very well. Don't worry. Tell steward to lock trunk in stateroom. Key is in small bag under my bed. Answer.—Signed, Florence C. Gerrish."

There was a minute's silence.

"It's over ten words," said Mrs Haddock.

Mrs Gerrish considered.

"I could leave out 'very,' 'is,' and 'my,' " she announced.

"It doesn't seem to say very much about the rest of us," said Mr Haddock.

"Of course I would pay for it myself," said Mrs Gerrish, and Mr Haddock blushed.

"Let me try writing a message," said Mrs Haddock, reaching for the pencil.

"Certainly—if you really think it will do any good," said Mrs Gerrish.

Mrs Haddock took the pencil and considered.

"Is bulkhead two words?" she asked.

"Are bulkhead two words?" corrected Mrs Gerrish. "Of course they are—at least they are where I come from."

"And water-tight?" asked Mrs Haddock.

"Of course," said Mrs Gerrish, condescendingly.

"Oh, dear," said Mrs Haddock, "what would you say in place of 'water tight bulk head'? "

They all considered carefully.

"Impervious something," said Mr Haddock. "Impervious——" and he looked at the captain.

Mr and Mrs Haddock Abroad

"There ought to be a code word for it," said Mr Haddock. "Captain, isn't there a code word for 'water-tight bulkhead'?"

The captain took a small book out of his pocket.

"Well," he said, "if you all seem determined to try this plan——" and he moistened his thumb and began turning over the pages of the book.

"What was the word?" he asked.

"Water-tight bulkhead," replied Mrs Haddock.

"Nothing here for 'water-tight,'" said the captain.

"Look under 'W,'" said Mr Haddock, so the captain looked under "W."

"Here it is," he said. "The code word for 'water-tight' is 'watigh' and for 'bulkhead' is —is—oh, here's the whole thing," he said. "'Water-tight bulkhead' is 'wabulk.'"

"There isn't any code word, is there," asked Mr Haddock, "which means 'Captain and Mr and Mrs Haddock and daughter and a Mrs Gerrish from Boston are in water-tight

[202]

bulkhead and would like to get out as soon as possible'?"

"What would that be under?" asked the captain.

"I was just joking," said Mr Haddock.

"This is hardly the time or the place to joke," said Mrs Gerrish, reprovingly.

"Here's my message," said Mrs Haddock, proudly. "It's only eight words," and she read:

"Look in wabulk for captain and four passengers."

"That leaves us two words yet," she said.

" 'Much love,' " suggested Mr Haddock.

"You couldn't say 'much love,' Will, unless you knew the person fairly well," said Mrs Haddock.

"By the way," asked Mrs Gerrish, looking at the captain, "whom shall we send it to?"

The captain took off his hat and scratched his head.

"It wouldn't look very well," he said, "for me to send it to any of the officers, because then they would think I really couldn't get out of here if I wanted to."

"Don't you want to?" asked Mr Haddock. "I mean—don't you want to get out of here?"

"Oh, sure," replied the captain, "but you don't understand how officers are."

"Well, then," said Mrs Gerrish, "let's send it 'To Whom It May Concern.' "

"All right," said Mrs Haddock, and she wrote that down. "We've still got those two words left, though."

" 'Am writing,' " suggested the captain.

"Am writing what?" asked little Mildred.

"A letter, of course," replied the captain, "and I think I've got a stamp, too."

"You'll pardon me for asking such a question at my age," said little Mildred, "but just how is this message going to get from here to 'To Whom It May Concern'?"

Everyone suddenly looked at everyone else and everyone else then suddenly looked at Mr Haddock.

"That was the one thing about my plan," he said, "that I wanted to ask you about."

Mr and Mrs Haddock Abroad

Mildred laughed—a dry, hollow laugh which echoed uncomfortably back and forth in the metallic vacuum of the bulkhead.

"All right," she said, "ask us."

There were several minutes of gloomy silence.

"My plan——" began the captain.

But just then, from way up above them, sounded once more a long shrill blast of the steamer's whistle.

And then, after a minute, the iron doors at each end of their prison slowly began to rise.

"Thank God," said Mr Haddock.

"Saved," said Mrs Gerrish.

"Mildred! come back here," said Mrs Haddock, "and let the older people go first. And *look* at the dirt on that dress."

But the captain detached himself as quickly as possible from Mrs Gerrish and went towards the door looking very unhappy.

"I'm sure I'm the only one," he muttered, "who's supposed to give that signal. It's in all the rules."

"And everybody knows it," he added.

[205]

"Oh, darn it," he said, and after he had bowed everyone out of the door he put on his cap and turned around and looked once more at his chalk diagram on the wall.

"I bet it might have worked," he said. "And now there'll just have to be another row."

"Oh, darn the old sea," he said, and he followed slowly and unhappily after the others, shuffling his feet along the iron deck as he went. "Oh, darn the old sea anyway."

CHAPTER VIII

"To-morrow will be Sunday," said the captain, late Saturday night.

"Ay, ay, sir!" said a sailor, saluting and backing out of the cabin.

And so, in accordance with the iron clad code of unquestioning obedience of those who go down to the sea in ships, the next day was Sunday.

And it was on Sunday, curiously enough, that the second class passengers revolted.

The history of this revolt is very interesting, especially for those who are interested in revolts. And for those who are not interested in revolts it is very interesting too.

So much for the history of the revolt.

"Wake up, Will," said Mrs Haddock, "it's Sunday."

"It is my invariable custom," replied Mr

Haddock, without opening his eyes, "to sleep late on Sunday morning."

"It *is* late," said Mrs Haddock. "They've moved the clock ahead another hour."

"Is that fair?" asked Mr Haddock, still half asleep. "Is that right? Is that in accord with those eternal principles——"

"Get up, Will!" said Mrs Haddock, in rebuttal.

"Where are the Sunday papers?" asked Mr Haddock, opening his eyes. "Mildred, go out and see if the papers have come yet."

But there were no Sunday papers, so after breakfast Mr Haddock went to divine service with Mrs Haddock and Mildred.

And divine service really wasn't divine service at all.

"This is just the lounging room," said little Mildred, who had an excellent memory for faces.

"Shhhh!" said Mr Haddock, "God is every-where on Sunday."

"He may be," said little Mildred, "but this is a good joke on Him, then, for these are certainly not the prayer-books we use at home."

"They aren't, are they, Will?" said Mrs Haddock.

"Of course not!" explained Mr Haddock.

"We will begin," announced the captain, who appeared to be conducting the service, "by singing Hymn 126. The one hundred and twenty-sixth hymn, 'For those in peril on the sea.'"

"That's a good one to start with," said Mr Haddock.

"Don't let father sing too loud," whispered Mildred to her mother, and Mrs Haddock smiled understandingly.

"You'll be careful of your throat, won't you, Will," she said to her husband. "Remember, you strained it last time."

"Oh, I guess I know what I'm doing," said Mr Haddock, and he took a deep breath, and Mrs Haddock and Mildred winced.

But when the ship's orchestra struck the opening notes of the hymn, Mr Haddock turned to his wife in dismay and said, "I guess I don't know that tune."

"Good!" cried little Mildred, and so the first hymn passed without incident.

"What kind of a church is this?" asked Mr Haddock, wonderingly to himself, but before anyone had time to answer, the captain was speaking again.

"My good friends——" he began, but just at that moment the ship suddenly came to a stop, throwing all the passengers out of their seats. Then, with much angry whistling, it began slowly to back in the general direction of America.

The captain picked himself up off the floor and put on his officer's cap.

"Who did that?" he asked angrily, and he pressed the nearest button. "And during divine service too!" But in order to reassure the somewhat doubtful passengers, the captain gave the signal for the orchestra to play another verse of Hymn 126, and at the conclusion of that stanza the lounge steward appeared, buttoning up his coat as he entered.

"You rang, sir?" he said, saluting.

"Your top button's unbuttoned," said the captain.

"Yes, sir!" said the steward, saluting once more.

"Well, fix it then, why don't you?" said the captain, peevishly, so the steward fixed it.

"Now," whispered the captain, "what's all this—this going backward and everything, during divine service?"

"I don't know, sir," said the steward; "Sunday is my day off."

"Well, send me somebody who does," said the captain, and turning to the congregation he said, "We will now sing another of our favourite hymns—Hymn 459—'Nearer, My God, To Thee.'"

"This service doesn't seem to be anything but hymns," said Mr Haddock.

Meanwhile the noise outside had increased in volume, and to the constant sound of the ship's whistles was added suddenly the tolling of several bells, much shouting, and the increasingly noisy popping of fire crackers.

"What is to-day?" asked the captain, looking for a calendar.

But before he had time to find one, the door burst open and a lone sailor appeared, wearing a bloody bandage around his head.

"The second class passengers," he gasped, pointing in the direction of the stern. "Not so loud," said the captain, putting his finger to his lips and motioning significantly to indicate the congregation.

"The second class passengers," whispered the sailor, "have revolted," and he fainted.

"Why?" whispered the captain, shaking the man gently, and then he muttered, "I bet it was that ham."

"My friends," said the captain, pulling the sailor furtively behind the desk so that no one could see him, "I'm afraid that divine service will have to be postponed for a few minutes owing to a last minute change in the plans of the program, necessitated by the unexpected illness of Mrs Gillette. However," he continued, gaining confidence, "we are fortunate in having among the passengers this morning

that well known amateur baritone and vocal-
ist, Mr P. T. Freeman, and Mr Freeman has
kindly consented to entertain you for a few
minutes with selections from his more than
extensive repertoire."

"Now, if you please, Mr. Freeman——"
said the captain, and Mr Freeman arose,
somewhat embarrassed, and with hands in
pockets and lowered eyes made his way to the
piano.

"I didn't bring my music," he said, unbut-
toning and buttoning his coat.

"Oh, that's all right, Mr Freeman," said the
captain, "we understand;" and then, turning
to the audience with a smile, he said, "And
I'm sure we'll all be very liberal towards Mr
Freeman's limitations, won't we?"

"Now then," said the captain, "if you'll
excuse me for a few minutes—and I'm sure,"
he said, "you will be in good hands—or
rather," he added, "in good voice. Ha, ha,
ha!" and he waved cheerily to Mr Freeman
and withdrew.

"I can do card tricks better than sing," announced Mr Freeman, after the captain had gone, "but if you would rather——"

"Do you know 'A Perfect Day?'" asked a lady in the front row. "'When you come to the end of a perfect day and you are alone with your thoughts'?"

"I know the *words*," said Mr Freeman.

"Maybe the pianiste knows the tune," suggested another passenger.

"Do you know 'A Perfect Day?'" asked the lady of the pianiste. "'When you come to the end of a perfect day and you are alone with your thoughts?'"

"I think so," said the pianiste. "Is this it?" and she struck a few opening chords.

"Oh, yes," said the lady, ecstatically. "Oh, please! Oh, let's have that!" So Mr Freeman cleared his throat, and sang "A Perfect Day."

"Oh, again!" cried the lady. "Oh, again! Oh, please, again!"

"What card tricks do you know?" loudly asked someone a little farther back.

"Do you think card tricks would be all right on Sunday?" asked Mr Freeman.

"Oh, sure!" cried an overwhelming number of voices. "Oh, perfectly all right."

"Better than singing?" asked Mr Freeman.

"Oh, much!" cried everybody, so instead of singing "A Perfect Day," Mr Freeman walked up to the platform and took a pack of cards from his pocket.

"Here you have a simple pack of fifty-two cards," he said, but just at that minute the ship stopped going backward just as suddenly as it had stopped going forward, and everyone looked at everyone else apprehensively.

"I take three cards——" said Mr Freeman, who had not noticed what had happened, "and put them in a trunk——"

But then the door opened and the captain re-appeared, looking somewhat worried.

"Ladies and gentlemen," said the captain, "you must pardon me just a little longer. Everything is all right and will be satisfactorily arranged if you will just have a little patience and bear with Mr Freeman's singing a little longer——"

"Have you got a trunk?" asked Mr Freeman, "and a globe of goldfish?"

"I'll have them sent right up," said the captain, and he added in a whisper, "Sing something not too heavy, Mr Freeman. Keep them entertained. You know—something like 'A Perfect Day.'"

"A trunk," said Mr Freeman, "and a globe of goldfish."

"Right!" said the captain, closing the door.

"I'll have to wait a minute," said Mr Freeman to the audience, "until I can get a trunk to put these cards in. Meanwhile," he said, "would any of you care to see a real Mexican rattlesnake watchfob?" And he took one from his pocket and passed it carefully along the front row.

"A real rattlesnake watchfob," he said. "That snake had eighteen rattles. Just pass it on back of you, please, to that lady—thank you."

"And here," said Mr Freeman, reaching in

an inside pocket, "is a lead bullet dug out of a telephone pole after the East St. Louis race riots, if you would care to see it," and that too was carefully passed around.

"Would you like to see some real tattooing?" asked Mr Freeman, and he took off his coat and rolled up his sleeves.

"That, madam," he said to an elderly lady in the front row, "was done in Baltimore. It's the American flag."

"Well, well!" said the lady. "The American flag. Well, well!"

"Would you care to see my chest?" asked Mr Freeman, but just at that moment two sailors arrived carrying a large empty trunk.

"Just put it there," said Mr Freeman, pointing to the platform.

"The captain says," explained one of the sailors, "that it will take ten or fifteen minutes for the—you know," and he whispered the words "goldfish globe."

"He thought maybe you could begin with this," said the other sailor, "and he said to be sure and not sing any mournful sort of songs for a while."

"All right!" said Mr Freeman, and stepping up on the platform he said, "Here we have a common ordinary trunk such as is often used in travelling. Quite empty," and he kicked the sides of the trunk and rapped on the lid.

"I wonder if that's our trunk," said Mrs Haddock.

"Now," said Mr Freeman, "I'm going to ask several of you to come up and examine this trunk carefully. Thank you!" And five or six of the passengers bashfully filed up to the platform and looked at each other and the trunk.

"Now," said Mr Freeman, producing a pair of handcuffs from his back pocket, "I'm going to ask you to handcuff me and put me in this trunk and lock the trunk securely."

"Aren't you going to sing 'A Perfect Day' again sometime?" asked the lady in the front row.

"Certainly," replied Mr Freeman, so he

was securely handcuffed and put in the trunk.
The lid was then clamped down and locked,
and everyone waited in breathless suspense.

But just then the captain re-appeared and
advanced solemnly to the front of the stage.

"Ladies and gentlemen," he said, "I regret
to announce that a very unforeseen happening
makes it absolutely impossible for us to continue this divine service any longer to-day. I
don't want any of you to be disappointed or
feel the least anxiety or apprehension about
anything, for I am sure that everything will
come out all right."

"What's wrong?" called a voice.

"Well, to make a long story short," said
the captain, "the second class passengers have
revolted. But we are arranging now for a
series of conferences and I am sure that everything will be satisfactorily adjusted in the
near future. Meanwhile," said the captain,
"I must ask you to be very careful of what you
eat and drink, and above everything else I
must ask you not to make any remarks which
might be taken the wrong way."

[219]

"But what are they revolting about?" asked a passenger.

"All that will be settled by conferences," replied the captain. "And now I must ask you to pass to your respective staterooms as quietly as possible."

And so the passengers one by one filed out of the lounge and went to their cabins, and it was not until two hours later that a sailor, who happened to come into the lounge in order to write some letters, heard a curious knocking near him, and upon investigation he discovered a trunk and upon opening that trunk he discovered a man with handcuffs on his wrists who seemed to be very apologetic and distressed, and who kept repeating the fact that it was very hot and uncomfortable in the trunk or otherwise he wouldn't have given up so soon.

During luncheon time there was an air of suppressed excitement in the dining room and after lunch, when Mr Haddock went to his stateroom for a short nap, he was awakened at the end of an hour by a knocking on his door.

"What is it?" he asked.

"The captain wants to see you right away," said the steward.

So Mr Haddock followed the steward up to the captain's cabin, and there he found four men seated opposite the captain at a large table.

"Come in, Haddock," said the captain, "we're in conference and need your advice."

"We don't at all," said one of the men across the table.

"Sit down, Haddock," said the captain, and he waved Mr Haddock into a vacant chair beside a man with a long beard.

"I object," said the man with a long beard.

"Mr Haddock," said the captain, "is an expert who has devoted his whole life to the study and investigation of conditions."

"He is not," said one of the gentlemen with a glare. "He doesn't know anything. His ignorance is colossal."

The captain smiled and shrugged his shoulders.

"Mr Haddock," he began again, "is the father of a family and the husband of Mrs Haddock."

"That's a lie," shouted all four in unison.

"Will you compromise on that?" the captain suddenly demanded.

There was a heated discussion and much excited whispering.

"Yes," their spokesman finally said, "if you will grant us Article 4."

The captain chewed the end of his pencil for a minute.

"Agreed," he finally said.

"Mr Haddock," he went on, "is at present on his way to Europe."

This remark threw the four into an uproar which lasted for several minutes. Finally they arose as one man and walked out of the cabin.

"We're through," they said. "This ends it."

The captain smiled after they had gone.

"They'll be back," he said. "Have a cigar."

"But what's it all about?" asked Mr Haddock.

"It's a conference," explained the captain.

"Oh!" said Mr Haddock.

In a few minutes the four returned.

"We'll agree to your last remark," they said, "if you'll agree to the present train schedule between Chicago and Milwaukee."

This was the captain's signal to leap from his chair.

"Never!" he shouted, and stormed out of the cabin.

"Have a cigar?" asked one of the four, of Mr Haddock.

"No, thanks!" said Mr Haddock. "I think I'd better be going."

"Oh, wait until the captain comes back," said the man. "He won't be long."

Finally the captain came back.

"All right," he said. "I'll accept the train schedule between Chicago and Milwaukee if you'll agree to the present arrangement of locks in the Panama canal."

The four looked at each other.

"All right," they said at last, and the captain wrote that down.

"That will do, Haddock," he said, "and thank you very much," and Mr Haddock, bowing to all, left the cabin.

"Where have you been?" asked Mrs Haddock, when he found her in her deck chair a few minutes later.

"I was called into conference," said Mr Haddock, as modestly as possible.

"How is it coming out?" asked Mrs Haddock.

"Oh, I think it will be arbitrated satisfactorily," said Mr Haddock.

And sure enough, after a short while, a long cheery blast of the whistle announced to the passengers that the whole difficulty had been satisfactorily cleared up by conference, and soon smoke was once more happily pouring from the huge funnels and the great steamship was once more merrily on its way toward Europe.

CHAPTER IX

And as the ship drew nearer and nearer to what the captain hoped would be France, the excitement of the passengers gradually increased, until on the last day there was no holding them back, and in spite of strict orders to the contrary many of them during the day foolishly jumped over the bow and began swimming ahead in their eagerness to set foot once more on land.

And their excitement was in no way diminished by the Ship's Concert, which came on the night before the last day.

"We have so much talent on board," said the captain to Mr Haddock on the morning of the concert, "that it's going to be difficult to get it all in, and I hate," said the captain, "to refuse anybody who is so nice as to volunteer."

"Let me see the program," said Mr Haddock, who by this time was on quite familiar terms with the captain.

"Well, first," said the captain, "I thought I would have a little music, and there's a lady on board—a Mrs Belden—who whistles beautifully, they say."

"That ought to be a good way to start," said Mr Haddock.

"Yes," replied the captain, "just the Star Spangled Banner and one encore—I asked her to make it fairly short. "Then," said the captain, consulting his list, "would come Bozo."

"Who?" asked Mr Haddock.

"Bozo," replied the captain. "She's sort of a weight lifter. I couldn't make it out very well—she doesn't speak much English. I'm pretty sure she's a weight lifter, though."

"I see," said Mr Haddock.

"Then," continued the captain, "we have a choice between Mr Freeman—you remember Mr Freeman——"

"Perfectly," said Mr Haddock, "and by the way, did he ever get out of that trunk?"

Mr and Mrs Haddock Abroad

"I think so," said the captain, "but we had better make sure," and he rang a bell.

"Find out," he said to the sailor who answered, "if a Mr P. T. Freeman is still on board. He might be in the trunk room," he added.

"Ay, ay, sir," said the sailor and he left, calling "Mr Freeman, please—Mr P. T. Freeman," as he went.

"A choice between Mr Freeman," continued the captain, "a lady named Iris Vance, and Dr Eliot Poindexter, the famous surgeon."

"You might combine them," suggested Mr Haddock.

"I thought of that," said the captain, "but Mr Poindexter says that he hasn't brought any of his surgical implements with him."

"That's too bad," said Mr Haddock. "A nice operation would be a novelty. What does Miss Vance do?"

"I don't know," said the captain, "she won't tell me. She just says, 'Oh, Captain, can't you guess!'"

"Well, can't you?" asked Mr Haddock.

"No," said the captain, "and she's so nice looking too."

"Maybe she's a ventriloquist," suggested Mr Haddock, "or a bearded lady. There's one who eats with us occasionally."

"She's not a bearded lady," said the captain, "I asked her."

"Then she's a ventriloquist," said Mr Haddock, "I know these women."

"I hate to leave Mr Freeman off," said the captain, "he was so nice yesterday."

"Maybe we can work him in later," said Mr Haddock, and they agreed on that.

"Then," said the captain, "we have the two Vernals."

"The two who?" asked Mr Haddock.

"The two Vernals," said the captain. "They do an act with pigeons."

"Would it be all right to shoot on board ship?"

"Shoot who?" asked the captain.

"The pigeons," replied Mr Haddock.

"I don't think it's that kind of an act," replied the captain. "I think the pigeons do tricks—fly around and sit on people's chests—you know."

"Like trained seals," said Mr. Haddock. "Sure. And by the way, are there any seals on board? There's a swell act."

"I don't think so," said the captain, "unless *that* is trained seals," and he pointed to a name on his list.

"No," said Mr Haddock. "It looks more like Martha Washington."

"It couldn't be her," said the captain. "She's dead."

"It might be a seal's name," said Mr Haddock. "They give seals awfully funny names some times."

"Don't they," said the captain, and they chuckled reminiscently.

"What else have you got?" asked Mr Haddock.

"Well," said the captain, "the rest of the acts don't sound as good. There's Lester A. Duffy."

"What's he do?" asked Mr Haddock.

"Boots and shoes," replied the captain. "He wants to give a talk about the leather business. He's got a lot of lantern slides which go with it."

"Lantern slides are very apt to crack," said Mr Haddock. "Who else?"

"Cameron J. Fiske," replied the captain. "He was the first white child born in Nevada."

"Can he do anything?" asked Mr Haddock.

"He can eat," replied the captain. "You ought to see him."

"That might make a good act for the children," said Mr Haddock.

"Then there's Mrs Earle," said the captain. "She's not very good looking, but they say she's very remarkable at burnt wood and leather, and she seems quite determined to help out."

"You've almost got enough now," said Mr Haddock.

"I know it," said the captain, somewhat despairingly. "And there's lots more who want to do things."

"We might put the names in a hat," suggested Mr Haddock, "and draw."

"Say, that's an idea," said the captain, brightening up, and they put twenty or thirty names on slips of paper and blindfolded a convenient sailor and had him draw out eight names, and when the captain read the eight names he looked gloomily at the barometer and said, "Well, we might as well go down to lunch," and so he and Mr Haddock went down to lunch.

"May I take off my blindfold now?" said the sailor, when they came back.

"Why, bless my soul," said the captain, "if I didn't forget," and he explained to the sailor how the concert was terribly on his mind, and the sailor was very nice about it and said he hadn't really cared a bit and the captain said, "Really?" and the sailor said, "No, really," and so the captain felt a whole lot better about it and gave all the sailors a double ration of grog that night, which made them feel very kindly toward the captain and toward each other and resulted in eight small fires, three cutting affrays, and a number of accidental drownings from overturned canoes.

And the passengers, too, made merry in their own way during dinner, and there was a great deal of popping of corks and informal crouching, so that by the time they had all assembled in the lounge for the concert they were in a rare holiday mood and the captain received quite an ovation when he stepped up on the platform in his uniform to announce the first number.

"The first number," he said, after the Star Spangled Banner had somewhat died down, "will be in the nature of a bedtime story by Miss Beatrice Gulick of the Denver Free Public Library."

"Hurrah," yelled a number of sailors, who were gazing in through the windows along the side, and the captain and audience smiled appreciatively at their enthusiasm.

"This evening——" began Miss Gulick, who by this time had reached the platform in a pink crêpe de chine.

"Oh—before I'd tell bedtime stories!"

THE SHIP'S CONCERT

"HURRAH," YELLED A NUMBER OF SAILORS, WHO WERE GAZING IN THROUGH THE
WINDOWS ALONG THE SIDE.

taunted a derisive voice somewhere in the rear, but he was quickly silenced by several disapproving "shushs" from his indignant neighbors, and Miss Gulick continued.

"This evening I am going to tell you the story of Johnny Skunk."

"Yeaaaa," cried the delighted sailors, "our favorite!" and Miss Gulick blushed with pleasure.

"Johnny Skunk," she began, folding her hands in front of her breast, "Johnny Skunk was in disgrace. And do you know why?"

"Yes," answered little Mildred, from the front row.

"Hush," said her mother.

"It was because," went on Miss Gulick, "he had lost his mittens."

"I bet it was," said little Mildred, more audibly than ever.

"Honest it was," said Miss Gulick, looking down at her. "Wasn't it, boys?" and she appealed to the sailors.

"Sure," they cried, "who says it wasn't?" and little Mildred wisely kept quiet.

"Yes, sir," went on Miss Gulick, "Johnny Skunk had lost his mittens. And where do you suppose he had lost them?"

"In Beatrice Beagle's bed-room," cried an eager sailor, who had heard the story many times by radio.

"That's right," said Miss Gulick. "He had left them in Beatrice Beagle's bed-room."

"Keep it clean," cautioned an elderly voice from the centre of the audience.

Miss Gulick flushed and walked to the front of the platform.

"I'm sure," she said, with her eyes snapping, "that there will be nothing in this story which any sailor wouldn't talk about in everyday conversation. Isn't that right, boys?"

"You bet it's right, Miss," they replied, and the audience applauded approvingly.

"Now then," she went on, "where were we?"

"In Beatrice Beagle's bed-room," they replied.

"That's right," said Miss Gulick, "and what do you suppose Johnny Skunk saw when

[236]

he went there the next night to look for his mittens?"

There was a silence and then one of the sailors held up his hand. "I know," he said.

"Yes?" said Miss Gulick, "and will you tell me?"

The sailor bobbed his head negatively several times.

"Please?" asked Miss Gulick.

"Go on, tell her, 'Dirty,'" said his fellow sailors.

"I'll have to whisper it to you," said the sailor, so he tiptoed through the door and up to the platform and whispered in Miss Gulick's ear.

Miss Gulick smiled, but shook her head.

"No, not that," she said, but she chuckled several times.

"Come here a minute," she said, beckoning with her finger, and the sailor returned.

"Did you hear the one——" began Miss Gulick, and she, in her turn, leaned over and whispered in the sailor's ear.

"Haw, haw, haw," roared "Dirty," when

she had finished, and he slapped his thigh heartily several times, while Miss Gulick smiled and the sailor returned to his place shaking his head and muttering, "Gee, that's a swell one."

"But Bobby Coon was watching all the time," said Miss Gulick, once more facing her audience, "and so Tommy Treetoad never found out after all what ailed Farmer Brown's dog. And that's why Billy Beaver was jealous."

And with that Miss Gulick smiled and unclasped her hands and bowed, and amid much applause from audience and sailors she returned to her seat.

"Now, boys," said the captain to the sailors, "bedtime."

"Oh, no, please," they cried. "It's only ten thirty."

"Oh, let them stay," said several, and Miss Gulick ran up to the captain and took his hand and said, "Please."

"All right," said the captain, "another half hour," and a great cheer went up and one ilor cried, "What's the matter with Miss Gulick?"

"She's all right," shouted his mates in unison.

"Who's all right?" he cried.

"Miss Gulick," was the deafening answer, and everybody clapped vigorously, while Miss Gulick pressed the captain's hand ever so slightly and sat down beside him and the captain was so pleased and delighted at the way the concert was going that he unconsciously patted Miss Gulick on the knee.

"Oh, captain!" called the sailors, "Oh, look at the captain!" and the captain, blushing furiously, pretended to be angry and said: "Now, men, that's enough," but everyone knew that he was not really very angry and no one was surprised when he later called one of his aides to him and gave orders that the sailors were all to be given another round of the ship's best grog.

"All the world's a stage," announced the captain, who was still blushing slightly as he arose, "and indeed those words of Shake-

speare are a happy omen for to-night, for
are very fortunate in having with us M
Emery J. Lothrop, who is interested in
amateur theatricals and indeed is practically
an actor, and so Mr Lothrop has kindly consented to give us the famous balcony scene
from 'Romeo and Juliet.' "

"Hamlet," whispered Mr Lothrop from the
door.

"Romeo and Juliet," repeated the captain.

"Hamlet," said Mr Lothrop more loudly.

The captain became quite irritated at this.

"Mr Lothrop," he said, "am I captain or
are you?"

"Hamlet," insisted Mr Lothrop, with two
bright red spots growing more intense on his
cheeks. "Hamlet."

"Let's take a vote on it," called a voice from
the audience.

"Mr Lothrop," said the captain decisively,
"there is no balcony scene in 'Hamlet,' and
you can ask anybody. Is there, men?" and he
appealed to the sailors.

"No!" they cried.

"You see," he said, turning to Mr Lothrop, "I want to be fair."

"Hamlet," said Mr Lothrop with grim determination.

"But Mr Lothrop, the balcony scene is in 'Romeo and Juliet,'" said the captain, trying to keep calm and patient.

"I never said anything about a balcony scene," said Mr Lothrop, defiantly.

"Why, Mr Lothrop!" said the captain, "you did, too."

"No, I didn't," said Mr Lothrop.

"Oh," said the captain; "well, that's different," and turning to the audience he cleared his throat and began: "All the world's a stage and indeed those words of Shakespeare are a happy omen for us to-night, for we have with us Mr Emery J. Lothrop, who will give us the famous scene from 'Hamlet,' and not the balcony scene from 'Romeo and Juliet,' because," and the captain, good "sport" as he was, could not refrain from "getting even" with Mr Lothrop just a little, "because, as we

all know, there is no balcony scene in 'Hamlet.' "

Mr Lothrop seemed nervous but defiant as
he mounted the platform.

"My friends," he said, "I want you to
imagine that this chair is a throne and over
here would be a doorway looking out on to
a courtyard. In that courtyard there would
be several linden trees. Then here," said he,
pointing to the piano, "would be two dormer
windows, half open. On the opposite side
there would be five marble pillars and another
door leading out into a long corridor. Now,
imagine all that scene carefully."

"Now," said he, changing his voice and retreating to the centre of the stage, where he
assumed a dramatic position, " 'To be or not
to be'—that is the question. Whether ' 'Twere
nobler to—to——,' " and then he stopped.

" 'To be or not to be,' " he began again,
" 'Whether 'twere nobler in the mind to—
to——' "

" 'To bear the slings and arrows of outrageous fortune,' " whispered one of the sail-

ors from the window nearest the stage.

"Oh, I know it," said Mr Lothrop.

"Well, why don't youse say it," answered the sailor.

" 'To be or not to be,' " began Mr Lothrop again. " 'That is the question. Whether 'twere nobler in the mind to bear the slings and arrows——,' " and once more he stopped.

" 'Of outrageous fortune,' " prompted the sailor, and some of the other sailors began stamping their feet and "booing" in a most discourteous manner and some even went so far as to shout "Let Miss Gulick do it!"

"Do you think I'd better?" whispered Miss Gulick to the captain, but just then Mr Lothrop said: "Captain, can't you do something about those men?" and the sailor who had been doing the prompting replied: "Say, come on out here, youse, and we'll 'do something about those men'," and Mr Lothrop said, "Do you dare me to come out?" and the sailor said, "Sure I dare you to come out." So Mr Lothrop took off his coat and coolly rolled up his sleeves and said to the audience: "Will you kindly excuse me for a minute while I administer a sound thrashing to this fellow?" and the audience applauded appreciatively while he walked through the door with a look in his eye which boded no good for a certain sailor, and after a few seconds there was a sound of scuffling and then what sounded very much like a splash, and the audience breathed a sigh of relief and the door opened and in walked the sailor.

"Would any of youse," he said, "like to hear Hamlet's soliloquy?"

And the audience, always fickle, applauded vigorously while the sailor mounted the platform and recited the soliloquy and his mates cheered him loudly at the end, as did also the passengers, and several of them came up to the platform to congratulate him, and one of them was a nice-looking lady who reached up and shook his hand and said, "You don't know me, but I'm Mrs Lothrop, and I enjoyed your talk ever so much, and I hope we can have you up in Montclair some time."

So the captain was more pleased than ever

at the success of his concert and he ordered another round of grog for the sailors and then stepped briskly upon the platform to announce the third number on the program.

"All of us," said the captain, "know Browning's justly famous poem, 'The Last Ride Together,' but few of us know that to-night we are fortunate in having with us Miss Minnie Canfield, champion lady bare-back rider of many states and for many years associated with the Barnum and Bailey circus."

This announcement created much excitement, and their curiosity reached a high pitch as the door swung open and in walked Miss Canfield, wearing a pale pink and lavender evening gown and carrying a small pearl-handled riding-whip.

"Unfortunately for many of us," said the captain, conducting the lady to the piano with a courtly bow, "Miss Canfield did not bring any of her horses with her on this trip, so she will sing in their place several old Scotch folk songs."

"In dialect," whispered Miss Canfield.

[245]

"In dialect," repeated the captain, and both were more or less right.

But at the end of the sixth song the unexpected extra ration of grog arrived for the sailors, and so great was their joy and appreciation that they began throwing bottles against the side of the ship and singing their own songs in competition with Miss Canfield, and when the captain attempted to remonstrate with them by saying "Careful, men!" they retaliated by shouting "We want Miss Gulick! We want Miss Gulick!" so that Miss Canfield was forced to cut her program short and omit all but the last eight songs in dialect, and during the last two of these the cries for "Miss Gulick" were almost deafening.

"Don't you think perhaps I had better go up and recite?" asked Miss Gulick of the captain, but he replied "No, I think they'll be all right after a while," so Miss Gulick sat down again.

But when the captain arose to announce Congressman F. P. Farnsworth, of Iowa, as Number 4 on the program, he only got as far as "It was Shakespeare, I believe, who first said 'Where the bee sucks there suck I,'" when two deck chairs came crashing through the nearest window, and that was the signal for the sailors to set up a steady chanting of "We want Miss Gulick" which, instead of diminishing, grew louder and more determined every minute, so that the captain was finally forced to give in and, amid deafening cheers, Miss Gulick arose and came forward to the platform.

"Do you really want me?" she asked with a modest coquettish smile, and an overwhelming "Yes" came from the sailors.

"Really and truly?" asked Miss Gulick, and their answer apparently removed her last lingering doubt, so she mounted the platform and the captain held up his hands for silence.

"Those of us," he said, "who remember Miss Gulick's first appearance on the platform will be happy to learn that, like the cat in the adage, she has consented to 'come back' and I therefore take great pleasure in introducing to this audience to which she needs no

introduction Miss Beatrice Gulick, of the
Denver Free Public Library, and," he added
in a happy after-thought, "like rain before
night, the sailors' delight."

"Oh, captain," said the "Sailors' Delight,"
and she roguishly gave him her hand, which
he took, blushing furiously, and the applause
lasted for several minutes.

"First of all," said Miss Gulick with her
eyes sparkling, "I wanted to propose three
cheers for our captain, Hip-hip——," and the
cheers were given with a will.

"Now, boys," she said, turning to the sailors, "which story do you want first?"

"Tommy Treetoad," cried the happy sailors, and so Miss Gulick told them the story of
Tommy Treetoad, and after that she told them
all the other bedtime stories that she knew,
and then, after three more cheers for the captain and three for Miss Gulick and three
times three for the International Society for
the Amelioration of the Condition of Mari-
time Widows and Orphans, or the "I. S. A. C.
M. W. O.," under whose auspices the enter-

tainment had been held, the concert was over and the stewards began clearing away the chairs in order that the dancing could begin.

"Don't leave me!" whispered the captain, clutching Mr Haddock's arm desperately as the guests were filing out of the room.

"Why?" asked Mr Haddock.

"Because——," said the captain, giving him a despairing look, but just then Miss Gulick spied him and came hustling up.

"Oh, captain," she said, "I'm sure you dance beautifully," and so, taking him by the arm, she led him away and that was the last Mr and Mrs Haddock saw of him that night, for they did not dance, themselves, and it was long past Mildred's bed-time, so they all went down to their stateroom and were soon fast asleep and dreaming of France.

CHAPTER X

The last day on board was passed very quietly by Mr and Mrs Haddock. Right after lunch Mrs Haddock began packing the steamer trunk.

"I don't see why you start packing so soon, Hattie," said Mr Haddock, lighting a cigar. "We aren't due to arrive till late to-night, and we won't leave the ship until to-morrow morning."

"Pass me those stockings of Mildred's," said Mrs Haddock, "and Will, I wish we could do something about all these nice empty preserve jars. Can't you put some of them in your bag?"

"No!" said Mr Haddock and he blew smoke thoughtfully out through the porthole. "Say, Hattie, I wonder what France is like?"

"Where's Mildred?" asked Mrs Haddock.

Mr and Mrs Haddock Abroad

"She's up on deck," said Mr Haddock; "playing with the boys."

"If she's with that Kaufman boy," said Mrs Haddock, "send her down to me."

"All right," said Mr Haddock, and he went out and up on deck, leaving his wife looking under the bed for his other grey sock.

Everyone seemed now to know everyone else, Mr Haddock noticed, and it made him feel good to have strange friendly people speak to him as he walked slowly along the deck. It was almost as though they all now shared some great secret which bound them together and made them all members of some fraternal organisation like the Masons back home.

Mr Haddock looked for the captain, but without success, so he walked around the deck eight times and then sat in his deck chair, lazily watching the people as they drifted or hurried by. There seemed to be a great many new ones—people he had never seen anywhere on board before.

"Well, we're almost there," he said to the

lady in the deck chair next him, but she was fast asleep, so he shook her until she woke up.

"Well, we're almost there," he said, as she finally opened her eyes.

"Where?" asked the lady, yawning.

"Europe," said Mr Haddock, and the lady turned her back on him and went to sleep again.

"I wonder what the captain's doing," said Mr Haddock to himself, and he watched carefully for Miss Gulick but she did not seem to be in the parade.

"I wonder what the captain's doing," he said, shaking the lady once more.

"I don't know," she replied somewhat crossly.

"Oh—were you asleep?" said Mr Haddock, and as she did not reply he leaned over and said very loudly: "I say, were you asleep?"

"Yes, I was!" she replied.

"Oh, pardon me!" said Mr Haddock.

After a while he yawned several times and then he began to whistle, and finally he got

Mr and Mrs Haddock Abroad

up and walked aimlessly until he came to the smoking room and sat down alone at a table in the corner.

"Haven't seen the captain, have you?" he asked the steward.

"No, sir," said the steward. "He hasn't been in to-day."

"Well, well," said Mr Haddock, and then he added: "Well, we're almost there, aren't we?"

"Yes, sir," said the steward, and Mr Haddock ordered a gin fizz.

"You interested much in baseball?" he asked the steward.

"No, sir," replied the steward.

"I'm not much of a fan, either," said Mr Haddock, and he sipped his drink.

"I see where that young cashier got twenty years for stealing those bonds," said Mr Haddock.

"I didn't read about it," said the steward.

"I feel kind of sorry for him," said Mr Haddock.

"A thief's a thief," said the steward.

[253]

"That's right!" said Mr Haddock, and he took another slow sip. "Yes, sir—you're certainly right."

"This has been a pretty good crossing, I imagine," said Mr Haddock.

"Not bad," said the steward.

"I suppose you get sort of used to it," said Mr Haddock.

"Yes, sir," replied the steward.

Mr Haddock finished his drink.

"Anything else, sir?" asked the steward.

"Not to-day," said Mr Haddock, jovially. "Next week, maybe!"

"Yes, sir," replied the steward, and Mr Haddock was left alone.

He drummed on the table several minutes with his fingers, then took his passport and some old letters out from his pocket and read them carefully several times.

"Ho hum!" said Mr Haddock, and he got up from his table and walked leisurely once more along the deck until he came to the library.

"Anything special, sir?" asked the library steward.

"No, thanks," said Mr Haddock, "I'll just look around."

"Yes, sir," said the steward, so Mr Haddock went slowly along the shelves reading the titles

When he had finished, he said to the steward: "There's a lot of books to read, aren't there?"

"Yes, sir," said the steward, and there was a silence.

"Haven't seen the captain, have you?" asked Mr Haddock.

"No, sir," said the steward.

Mr Haddock started back along the shelves until he reached the door.

"Well—good day!" he said to the steward. "I guess I won't take anything, after all."

"Good day, sir," said the steward, and he returned to his book.

Mr Haddock wandered down to his stateroom.

"Well, Hattie," he said, "we're almost there."

"Did you see Mildred?" asked his wife.

"No," he said, "but she's all right."

"Why don't you lie down a bit, Will?" said Mrs Haddock. "Here—I'll take those things off your bunk."

So Mr Haddock lay down and closed his eyes and soon was fast asleep, and he slept until Mildred came down and woke him up for dinner time.

Dinner was quite exciting. "I think we ought to order a bottle of champagne," said Mr Haddock.

"Now, Will!" said Mrs Haddock.

"It's the last night," said Mr Haddock, so he ordered a bottle of champagne, which seemed to please the waiter very much.

"Here's to you, Hattie!" he said, and he drank to Mrs Haddock, and she drank to him, and little Mildred was allowed to have a small glass.

"Not bad," was the little girl's comment.

"You'll get to like it," said Mr Haddock,

[256]

"if you just keep at it," and he made as if to pour his glass into his daughter's.

"Now, Will," said Mrs Haddock.

"I was just joking," said the head of the family, but when Mrs Haddock was looking under the table for her napkin he did reach over and pour a very little into Mildred's glass.

Then the other three people at their table, whom Mr and Mrs Haddock had hardly laid eyes on since the first day, unexpectedly arrived and Mr Haddock asked them to share his champagne, and they immediately bought two more bottles, so that by the time dinner was over all were very merry and Mr Haddock was telling his famous story about his fishing trip in Wisconsin.

"I swear, Will," said Mrs Haddock, as they were walking up the stairs after dinner, "I believe I'm a little tipsy. Take my arm."

"Ho! Ho! Ho!" laughed Mr Haddock; "you old souse!"

"Sh——," said Mrs Haddock, looking around, and she gave him her arm and they

walked quietly around the deck several times
and then sat down in their deck chairs.

"Where's Mildred?" asked Mrs Haddock,
after Mr Haddock had lighted his cigar.

"She's all right just where she is," said Mr
Haddock. "Now, don't get up, Hattie. Let's
sit here quietly for a while."

"I'll bet she's with that Kaufman boy," said
Mrs Haddock.

And as a matter of fact, Mildred was with
the Kaufman boy.

"That's some moon!" said the Kaufman
boy.

"I'll say it is," said Mildred.

There was a silence.

"Say, Mildred," said the Kaufman boy.

"What, Morris?" said Mildred.

"Are you going to write to me?" asked
Morris.

"Sure!" said Mildred. "Morgan Harjes—
Paris."

"That's right!" said Morris, "and I'll write
to you—American Express."

Again there was a silence.

"That's sure some moon," said Morris.

"I'll say it is," said Mildred.

"Mildred!" came the sound of a voice—Mrs Haddock's voice.

"All right!" yelled Mildred, and soon Mr Haddock's cigar came forward through the darkness.

"I know a little girl who's sleepy,"_said Mr Haddock.

"I don't," said Mildred, but she said "Good-night" to Morris and went with her parents to their stateroom.

"That champagne made me drowsy, Will," said Mrs Haddock, yawning.

"Oh, come on—stay up and see the lights of France," said her husband.

"That might not be for hours," said Mrs Haddock, beginning to undress.

"I think I'll go up on deck and smoke another cigar," said Mr Haddock. "I might find the captain."

But he did not find the captain and so, after finishing his cigar, he tossed it way out into the ocean and watched it disappear and then he stood for a long time looking out over the water, after which he went slowly around the deck once more and then downstairs and to bed.

He did not know how long he had been asleep when he was awakened by a tapping on the door.

"Will!" said Mrs Haddock, who was a light sleeper, "somebody's knocking. Will—wake up!"

"Who's there?" called little Mildred.

"Is that Mr William Haddock?" whispered a voice.

"Yes," said Mr Haddock.

"The captain would·like to see you right away," said the voice.

"Now, Will," said Mrs Haddock, "don't you go drinking and staying up all night."

"I won't," said Mr Haddock, "maybe he needs me," and he began to dress.

"This way, sir," whispered the sailor when he opened the door, and Mr Haddock followed.

"It's quite a ways, sir," said the sailor, helping Mr Haddock down an iron ladder, and a few minutes later he said, "This here is about twenty feet under the sea."

Finally they reached a good sized place full of boxes and bales.

"All right, Sir," called the sailor switching on his electric torch, and from behind a pile of trunks slowly and cautiously appeared the captain.

"Good evening, Haddock," said the captain.

"Good evening, Captain," said Mr Haddock, and the sailor left them alone.

"Well, Captain——" began Mr Haddock.

"Shhh——" said the captain and he went over and pulled the bolt in the door.

"What's the trouble?" asked Mr Haddock.

The captain did not reply at first.

"Everything going all right up above?" he asked Mr Haddock.

"Oh, sure," said Mr Haddock, "we ought to be in port soon."

"I hope so," said the captain, "gosh, I certainly hope so."

Mr Haddock took out a cigar and slowly bit off the end.

"Is it a woman?" he asked.

The captain hesitated and then nodded.

"Can you smoke here?" asked Mr Haddock, and then he added, "Miss Gulick?"

The captain shuddered.

"Yes," he said.

Mr Haddock lighted his cigar.

"What did you do to her?" he asked.

"Nothing," protested the captain, "absolutely nothing. That's just it, Haddock."

"Well now, Captain," said Mr Haddock, "we might as well be frank about this; I'm not going to give you away."

"Honest," replied the captain, "so help me God, I haven't done anything to that terrible woman."

"Well, then," said Mr Haddock, "how did you get in for this?"

"I don't know," replied the captain. "That's just it, I don't know. All I know is that ever since the concert last night she has been following me around and taking me by the arm and honest to God, Haddock, I'm desperate. I don't know what to do. Here we are getting into port and I ought to be on the bridge in my uniform when we get in so they can see me from land, and here I've spent all afternoon and night down here in this loathsome place just because every time I go up on deck she's watching to take me by the arm, and honest to God, Haddock, I'm desperate."

Mr Haddock slowly rolled his cigar around in his mouth.

"Well," he said at length, "women are funny."

"Funny as hell," said the captain, and they both lapsed into silence.

"Now if she was a woman like Mrs Haddock," said Mr Haddock at length, "I'd say 'go right ahead!'"

"Go right ahead what?" asked the captain.

"Marry her," replied Mr Haddock.

"But I don't want to marry her," objected the captain; "her or anybody."

"I don't know as I blame you," said **Mr** Haddock. "Marriage is a funny thing."

"If you get the right girl," he went on, "marriage is the greatest thing in the world. If you get the wrong girl, it can be hell.

"Now if Miss Gulick was like Mrs Haddock——"

"She isn't," said the captain; "she isn't like anybody. And I don't see why she can't let me alone so I can be on the bridge when we come into harbor. I don't see why she has to spoil this whole trip. I never met her before last night, anyway. I can't tell you, Haddock," he cried, "how I hate to have women paw me."

"That's one good thing about Mrs Haddock," said Mr Haddock. "No matter how——"

"But what am I going to do?" interrupted the captain. "What am I going to do?"

"Well," said Mr Haddock, "I don't know. When Mrs Haddock and I were first married——"

"But I tell you I don't want to get married,"

cried the captain. "Honest, Haddock, I'm
perfectly happy."

"You think you are," said Mr Haddock,
"but wait till you've been married a while—
say, captain, you don't know what happi-
ness is."

"All right," said the captain, "but what I
would like to know is—how am I going to get
up on the bridge without her seeing me?"

Mr Haddock knocked a long ash off onto
the cement floor. "Well," he said at last, "I
might go on ahead—and if she's not waiting
there I'll come back and tell you."

"And if she *is* waiting?" asked the captain.

"I'll go on to bed," said Mr Haddock.

The captain plunged his hands through his
hair.

"If she *is* there," he said, "I'm going to do
something desperate. Haddock," he said,
"I'm going to do something desperate."

"I wouldn't do that," said Mr Haddock,
and he got down off his box and stamped on
the butt of his cigar. "Now remember, if she

is there, I'll not come back—but don't you do anything foolish."

The captain did not reply, so Mr Haddock patted him once or twice on the shoulder and left.

And just as he emerged onto the upper deck he met Miss Gulick.

"You haven't seen the captain, by any chance, have you?" she asked. "I know somebody who's looking for him."

"No," said Mr Haddock, "I haven't seen him," and he walked along the empty deck and down the main stairway and into his stateroom.

"What was it, Will?" asked Mrs Haddock.

"Nothing you'd understand," replied her husband, and he looked at his watch. "You could see the lights along the shore of France," he added.

He lay there for some time, feeling the engines throbbing way down below him near where he had left the captain.

"I hope he doesn't do anything foolish," he murmured.

Mr and Mrs Haddock Abroad

Then the steady measured rhythm of the driven ship slowly lulled him towards sleep and he closed his eyes. And just before dropping off he imagined for a minute that he heard rapid running footsteps on the deck overhead, and then a splash, and the distant, monotonous call of a sailor on watch: "Captain o-over-board!"

But he wasn't sure and he was very sleepy and very tired, and when he opened his eyes again the ship had stopped and the sun was streaming through the porthole and the steward was knocking on the door.

"Europe, sir!" cried the steward. "Europe."

The Haddocks had arrived.

THE END

Afterword

by Donald Ogden Stewart

The actual writing of this book took place in Paris during the spring and summer of 1924 when I was approaching my thirtieth year and had already published three books (one each year since I had unexpectedly become a writer in 1921). I use the word "unexpectedly" as I had been graduated from Yale in 1916 with the not unusual ambition (for a Yale man) of becoming president, or at least vice-president, of a bank or a bond-selling establishment in Columbus, Ohio (where I had been born) or in some equally fortunate city which I had selected for my successful financial career.

But — things didn't quite turn out that way and I found myself in New York City in 1921 without any money or any particular prospects of making any — a very unusual situation in those days for a Yale man. Fortunately, in the interim, I had made the acquaintance of a young Princeton graduate named F. Scott Fitzgerald who had an ambition to become a novelist and had written a recently published book called *This Side of Paradise* which seemed to me not a bad book for a Princeton man to have written. Anyway, Scott sent me in my despair to a magazine called *Vanity Fair* where two of his classmates,

Afterword

Edmund Wilson and John Peale Bishop, were editors, to see if I might perhaps get a job in the advertising department. Scott also suggested that I take with me a sample of something I had written and as unfortunately there didn't happen to be any samples, I wrote a parody of *This Side of Paradise* which, to Scott's and my surprise, they liked. And, furthermore, they made the astounding suggestion that I give up trying to be president of a bank and become a writer of parodies and other bits of humour.

So that was the beginning of my career as a writer, and by 1924 the publishing firm, George H. Doran, had had the courage to publish three of my books, in the last one of which *(Aunt Polly's Story of Mankind)*, I had intended to show that I was not only a writer of humourous parodies but also a serious critic of various incorrect economic and political tendencies of the capitalistic world. Unfortunately, poor dear *Aunt Polly* laid more or less of a rather unsuccessful egg and it was in more or less of a discouraged mood that I found myself on the Left Bank in Paris in the spring of 1924 wondering what in hell to write my next book about.

Fortunately, however, during the preceding winter I had been asked by the Authors' League to make a contribution to the gaiety of their annual banquet and even more fortunately, I had made the friendship of Robert Benchley, Marc Connelly and Ring Lardner, and it is to these three

Afterword

(especially to Ring, God bless him), that I particularly owe the creation of Mr and Mrs Haddock and their daughter Mildred. A short time before the aforementioned Authors' League banquet Ring had written a marvelous piece called *I Gaspiri — or The Upholsterers* which had introduced me to what was beginning to be known as "Crazy Humour." So at the banquet, Bob, Marc and I let go (accompanied by Bob on his mandolin) with some more and some crazier humour which seemed to hit the right spot.

Anyway, when I found myself in Paris in 1924 I decided to abandon momentarily the reform of capitalistic civilisation in favour of something more resembling *Alice in Wonderland* or the Marx Brothers and out of that, with much enjoyment, emerged *Mr and Mrs Haddock Abroad*. It was terribly easy to write (sitting in my little room at the Hotel Montparnasse) and what was even more fun was to trot every evening with what I had written over to the Place St. Michel where Gerald and Sara Murphy were living and where the audience of listeners usually included their friends Ernest and Hadley Hemingway, John Dos Passos, and Gilbert Seldes, aided by certain magic drinks which Gerald and Sara devised.

And that, dear readers, is the history of the writing of this book and of one of the happiest summers that I have ever enjoyed.

Textual Note

The text of *Mr. and Mrs. Haddock Abroad* published here is an exact photo-offset reprint of the first printing (New York: Doran, 1924). No emendations have been made in the text.

M. J. B.

Lost American Fiction Series

published titles, as of October 1975
please write for current list of titles

Arbuthnot - 144 (Rod Suellian doc et yrs)